Praise for Tim Myers's Candlemaking Mystery series

Death Waxed Over

"Excellent storytelling that makes for a good reading experience . . . [Myers] is a talented writer who deserves to hit the bestseller lists." —*The Best Reviews*

Snuffed Out

"A sure winner." —Carolyn Hart, author of the Death on Demand series

"An interesting mystery, a large cast of characters, and an engaging amateur sleuth make this series a winner." —*The Romance Reader's Connection* (four daggers)

At Wick's End

"A smashing, successful debut." —*Midwest Book Review*

"I greatly enjoyed this terrific mystery. The main character . . . will make you laugh. Don't miss this thrilling read." —*Rendezvous*

"A clever and well-done debut." —Mysterylovers.com

continued . . .

A POUR WAY TO DYE

TIM MYERS

BERKLEY PRIME CRIME, NEW YORK

THE BERKLEY PUBLISHING GROUP
Published by the Penguin Group
Penguin Group (USA) Inc.
375 Hudson Street, New York, New York 10014, USA

Penguin Group (Canada), 90 Eglinton Avenue East, Suite 700, Toronto, Ontario M4P 2Y3, Canada
(a division of Pearson Penguin Canada Inc.)
Penguin Books Ltd., 80 Strand, London WC2R 0RL, England
Penguin Group Ireland, 25 St. Stephen's Green, Dublin 2, Ireland (a division of Penguin Books Ltd.)
Penguin Group (Australia), 250 Camberwell Road, Camberwell, Victoria 3124, Australia
(a division of Pearson Australia Group Pty. Ltd.)
Penguin Books India Pvt. Ltd., 11 Community Centre, Panchsheel Park, New Delhi—110 017, India
Penguin Group (NZ), Cnr. Airborne and Rosedale Roads, Albany, Auckland 1310, New Zealand
(a division of Pearson New Zealand Ltd.)
Penguin Books (South Africa) (Pty.) Ltd., 24 Sturdee Avenue, Rosebank, Johannesburg 2196,
South Africa

Penguin Books Ltd., Registered Offices: 80 Strand, London WC2R 0RL, England

This is a work of fiction. Names, characters, places, and incidents either are the product of the author's imagination or are used fictitiously, and any resemblance to actual persons, living or dead, business establishments, events, or locales is entirely coincidental.

PUBLISHER'S NOTE: The recipes contained in this book are to be followed exactly as written. The publisher is not responsible for your specific health or allergy needs that may require medical supervision. The publisher is not responsible for any adverse reactions to the recipes contained in this book.

A POUR WAY TO DYE

A Berkley Prime Crime Book / published by arrangement with the author

PRINTING HISTORY
Berkley Prime Crime mass-market edition / August 2006

Copyright © 2006 by Tim Myers.
Cover design by Annette Fiore.
Interior text design by Kristin del Rosario.

ISBN: 0-425-21115-0

BERKLEY® PRIME CRIME
Berkley Prime Crime Books are published by The Berkley Publishing Group,
a division of Penguin Group (USA) Inc.,
375 Hudson Street, New York, New York 10014.
The name BERKLEY PRIME CRIME and the BERKLEY PRIME CRIME design are trademarks belonging to Penguin Group (USA) Inc.

PRINTED IN THE UNITED STATES OF AMERICA

10 9 8 7 6 5 4 3 2 1

As always,
to Patty and Emily.
My reasons why.

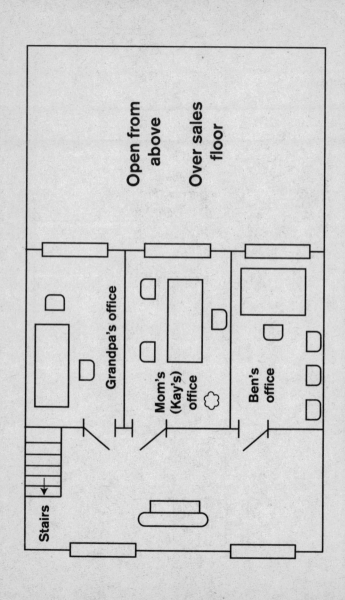

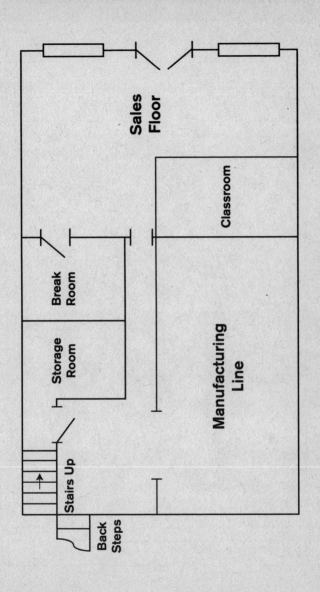

PROLOGUE

o o o

FOR a man named Joy, there was clearly none left in his lifeless body. Lying on the floor near the tub—one arm outstretched before him—he clutched a scented bar of soap in his left hand. It wasn't Dove or Lifebuoy or Dial, but a handcrafted cleanser, wrapped with the label, Where There's Soap, which was made in the shop that abutted his jewelry store's property. Though it is true that more accidents happen in the bathroom than any other room in the house, this was no accident. Someone had clubbed him from behind with the iron bar from a towel rack and then left him for dead.

After the attack, Joy had only a little life remaining—not enough to call for help or even to linger more than a few moments—so he had to act quickly while he still could. He grabbed the only thing within reach that might help name his killer, if only the police were smart enough to discover the clue he was leaving behind.

.

ONE

○ ○ ○

THE DAY BEFORE

I had to slam on my Miata's brakes to keep from plowing through a chain-link fence as I started to pull into the back parking lot of my family's soap factory and boutique, Where There's Soap. I wasn't being reckless or driving impaired; that fence hadn't been there when I'd left the night before. I somehow managed to stop before I rammed into the thing, but just barely. As I shut off the engine, I tried to slow my pounding heart. What kind of foolishness was this? Then I saw the sign wired to the eight-foot-high fence. It told me everything I needed to know. Earnest Joy was at it again, only this time he'd gone too far.

MY name is Benjamin Perkins, and my family and I run the largest custom soapmaking production line and boutique in our part of North Carolina. My three sisters teach most of the classes and handle the customers in front, while my three brothers run the production line in back. Our mother oversees us all, with our grandfather popping in every now and then to add his opinions to the mix. That leaves me the hardest job of all, in my opinion. At thirty-three, I'm the family and business troubleshooter. Whenever there's a problem, it's up to me to fix it. And believe me, there's always a problem. Most folks are surprised when they find out a guy like me—six feet tall and 180 pounds—is a soapmaker by trade, but it's the family business, and like it or not, I'm usually right in the middle of everything going on at Where There's Soap. When I'm not trying to keep our little world safe and sane, I teach a few soapmaking classes in the classroom up front and even help my brothers on the production line now and then. As the eldest of seven children, I stepped into my father's role the day he died, and I haven't had a quiet moment to myself since.

It appeared that today wasn't going to offer any tranquility either.

I tested the fence and found that it was solid, its posts buried in the ancient blacktop surface of our lot. I left the Miata where it was and started off on foot toward the source of our trouble. In all honesty, I was too angry to drive, and Earnest Joy's jewelry store was close by, situated on land that abutted ours. I took the sidewalk, never even thinking of cutting across the grassy lawn between us. Earnest wouldn't have allowed it before, but now there was an even bigger reason besides him and his fence. His son Andrew—a young man who had never shown a real interest in anything in his life—had suddenly decided he wanted, more than anything else in the world, to become a master gardener, converting every square inch of green into growing something. As I looked over his straggly crops, I realized that passion and excellence don't always go hand in hand. It appeared that as soon as Andrew dug up a bit of dirt, he haphazardly threw a handful of seeds into the ground and then started on a new section. I had to give him credit for one thing. He'd plowed into the hobby with a zeal that amazed me.

I wasn't the least bit surprised to find Earnest Joy waiting for me near the door inside his handcrafted jewelry store when I walked up, though I could see from the sign that he wasn't due to open for another hour and a half. No doubt he'd been there since dawn, eagerly anticipating another clash with me and my family. I liked to think the Perkins clan had a "live and let live" approach to life, but when it came to our back door neighbor, I'm afraid our best intentions faltered now and then. Earnest certainly didn't make it any easier on us, constantly goading and prodding us with backhanded compliments and disdainful looks. Most of the time it felt like his motivation for aggravation was pure sport alone, but this time he'd crossed the line. He'd elevated our conflict from a brush war to an all-out attack.

Before I could say a word, I noticed that another man was in the shop with him, lurking near the back with his chair balanced on its back two legs, though with his bulk, I thought it was a precarious way to sit. I'd seen him around town—Harper's Landing wasn't all that big a place—but as far as I knew, our paths had never crossed before. He sat there staring at me, his pale moon face smiling with a picket fence grin. I shook my head—dismissing his presence—and turned to Earnest Joy. If he wanted an audience, that was fine with me.

"Have you completely lost your mind?" I asked, fighting to keep my voice below a bellowing rage.

Joy said snidely, "Perkins, I'm afraid I'm going to have to ask you to leave." His gaze stayed on the ledger he was pretending to study as he spoke, but I could see a smile start to blossom on his face. "I'm not open to the public right now," he added, then he gestured to his friend. "This is a private meeting we're having right now, isn't it, Ralph?"

The other man, testing the seams of his flannel shirt and canvas pants with his immensity, said smugly, "That's right, no visitors allowed."

"You can't be serious," I said as I stared at Joy, fighting to keep my temper in check. Earnest was a heavyset man, though he looked absolutely lithe compared to his friend Ralph. Joy sported a hairline that retreated farther than the French Army and a scowl that appeared to be permanently attached to his less-than-handsome mug.

"If you can't be civil, I'll call the law on you. Try me and see."

He meant it, too. We'd been adversaries since I was a kid, when one of my errant pitches to a brother had the misfortune of crossing his property line while he was out patrolling the grounds. He'd gleefully confiscated our ball, refusing to give it back no matter how much we'd pled, and I'd had an intense dislike for the man ever since.

My first reaction at the moment was to scream at him about the fence he'd put up and marked as Joy Property, but I knew that was his wildest desire. So, instead of shouting, I took a few dozen deep breaths and looked around his shop until I could say something below the decibel level of an angry chainsaw. Earnest, along with his son and daughter's help on occasion, ran a shop stocked with jewelry they made themselves. While I'd never cared for Earnest Joy, even I had to admit that he had a delicate touch with silver and gold, marrying them to precious and semiprecious stones with an artisan's skill and a master's touch. There were pieces that incorporated gold and silver coins in their design, and some that sparkled with small diamonds and emeralds. No doubt his shop would have been better suited in a city bigger than our small town, but from the look of prosperity around the place, it appeared that he managed to do just fine in Harper's Landing.

I was still trying to keep my temper when Earnest looked up from his ledger and stared directly at me, no doubt wondering if I'd suddenly been struck mute. "If you've got something to say, spit it out, boy. I don't have all morning. I know there's got to be some reason you're here so early."

I suddenly realized that if I waited until my blood pressure retreated to a normal level, I'd be standing there for the rest of my life. Keeping my voice as calm as I could, I said, "You know why I'm here. We need to talk about that fence. What were you thinking when you had it put up? Were you drunk?"

That brought a wicked little smile to his face. "I decided to finally lay claim to what's rightfully mine. Your family has been squatting on my property long enough. I own every inch of the land that runs right to the back edge of your building. Just be glad it didn't touch the place itself, or I'd have that old rattrap torn down to the ground, at least as much of it that stood on my land."

"I don't believe it," I said fiercely.

He snarled, "Don't doubt it for one second. The bulldozers would be out there so fast you wouldn't even have time to grab a bar of soap before I knocked the place down."

Ralph thought that quip was hilarious, but I was focused on Earnest. It was all I could do not to shake him silly.

"I know you'd tear our place down if you could, but that land belongs to us."

"Are you calling me a liar, Ben?" Earnest asked in a serpentine voice. "I've got the papers right here if you don't believe me. I just had it surveyed, and it's all legal as can be."

He handed me a stapled document, and I studied it. There was a drawing taking up most of the top sheet, along with a set of coordinates that didn't make the slightest bit of sense to me. In addition, there were several pages of legalize attached that read like bad Lewis Carroll. The map was clear enough, though. I saw the line drawn just at the edge of our building. If it was true, it would kill us. Not only did all of the Perkins clan park in back—a substantial number of vehicles given nine family members who didn't believe in carpooling—but it was where we received our deliveries and shipped our soaps out into the world. Without access to the back of our building, I didn't see how we could operate for very long. I started to tear the document up, as if that would make the problem go away. Earnest must have guessed my intentions.

"That's a copy I had made especially for your grandfather. Ask him if it's not true." His smug confidence made my belief in his insanity falter for a second. Could it be that for once in his life, Earnest Joy wasn't lying to me? Was there something I didn't know about all of this?

I'm not a violent man by nature, but at that moment, I wanted to take a swing at him. Somehow I managed to fight the impulse. It was time to get more information before I gave Earnest Joy yet another reason to dislike us. It was pretty obvious by the expression on his face that he'd expected a shouting match or even an errant punch, and I took a little comfort in at least denying him that.

I tapped the sheaf of papers with the back of my hand, then said as I left, "This isn't over. I'll be in touch."

If I didn't dislike Earnest so much at that moment, I actually might have felt sorry for him. It appeared that I'd robbed him of his eagerly anticipated glee by not reacting to his overt aggression. Well, that was something, anyway.

I ran into his daughter, Terri Joy, on the porch as I was leaving. Terri was my age, rail thin, and had frizzy red hair. She was dressed rather stylishly in a dark tailored outfit that looked expensive; I knew dressing well had always been important to her. While many of the kids had teased her growing up about her hair and lack of a real figure, I'd always been fond of her. She was smart, and had a wit as sharp as honed steel that she used to defend herself from our peers.

Terri frowned the second she saw me, honest regret in her gaze. "Ben, I'm so sorry. I had no idea he was going to put that fence up. I just found out about it myself."

Terri and I had always gotten along reasonably well—an aberration in the long-standing family feud—though unlike Romeo and Juliet, we'd never been anything but friends. "Can't you at least talk some sense into him?"

Terri shook her head. "I wish I could, but the two of them are being even more stubborn than usual. Lately, Andrew's been behaving as badly as Dad. I'm so sorry, but there's nothing I can do about it. You know how they both are."

I nodded. "I understand, Terri. It's not your fault. I don't blame you."

"I truly am sorry," she said. "I hope this doesn't ruin our friendship."

"Me, too," I said as I walked away.

I left her on the jewelry store's steps and started back toward the soap shop. It was time to find my grandfather and see if Earnest Joy was telling the truth. Like everyone else in the family, I'd assumed all my life that the land in question belonged to us, but now Joy was saying otherwise, and he'd implied that the reason was because of my grandfather. I loved Paulus, but he wasn't an easy man to get along with. My grandfather hated to be questioned by anyone, particularly someone from the family. Interrogating him was a prospect I didn't relish, but it had to be done, and the sooner the better.

By the time I got back to the soap shop, Mom was just pulling in beside my car on the tiny island of pavement in front of the fence. There had barely been enough room for me to get the Miata off the road, so my mother's minivan was halfway out in the turn lane when she stopped. At least she'd managed to keep from hitting the fence, or me, for that matter.

Ignoring a bleating horn behind her, my mother got out and looked at me severely. "Benjamin, what's the meaning of this?"

"Hey, don't blame me, I didn't put it up."

She rolled her eyes as she shook her head, obviously showing disdain for her eldest child's intelligence. "I know that. What happened?" She approached the sign and read it aloud. " 'PROPERTY OF EARNEST JOY. NO TRESPASSING.' Has that man finally lost what little of his mind he had left?"

A car drove by and honked its disproval of my mother's parking job with a steady blast as it barely missed the rear end of her vehicle.

I suggested, "Why don't you pull into the customer parking lot and then we can discuss this."

She shook her head. "If the entire family parks there, we'll have no room for our customers." She had a point.

There were days when we had more Perkins offspring at Where There's Soap than customers.

"Look on the bright side. It will certainly look like we're busy all the time." She was ready to reply when I cut her off, a dangerous thing in the best of times. "Mom, why don't we both move our vehicles and then I'll tell you all about it. I promise."

I wasn't sure if she'd do as I asked, but thankfully she got into her minivan and backed up into the street, nearly hitting a brand-new Mercedes in the process. After both our vehicles were safely ensconced in the customer lot on the side of the shop, I said, "Earnest claims that the land all the way to the back of our building belongs to him. He just had a new survey done."

Mom asked, "Did you happen to see the name of the surveyor?"

I thought about it a second, then said, "Don't quote me, but I think it said 'Monk.' " I dug the document out of my back pocket and handed it to her.

Mom shook her head as she accepted it from me. "Try Thunk. David Thunk."

"Yeah, you're right. It is Thunk. I've never heard of the guy."

My mother frowned as she stared at the papers, then said, "I wish I could say the same. He and Earnest go way back. They've been lying and cheating for each other for years. I suppose that the thing that amazes me the most is that he didn't try this sooner. The two of them would steal the shoes off a baby's feet without a second thought."

I didn't want to bring my grandfather's name up since he and my mother had been squabbling the last time they'd been together, but I didn't have much choice. Besides, how much angrier could she get?

"Grandpa's involved somehow," I admitted.

Man oh man, had I been wrong. There was a new intensity to her glare as she spat out her words. "What did he do, lose our land in a card game, or was it betting on a coin toss? No, he probably lost it playing checkers. Paulus is reckless, Ben. He always has been. And now it's going to ruin us."

My grandfather was my father's father, and when Dad was alive, he and my mother appeared to get along just fine. After Dad died, though, the tension between them started to grow, and Paulus had mentioned loudly on several occasions that my mother was running the family business into the ground. It was clearly up to me to fix this, if I could.

"We need to talk to him to find out what's really going on, Mom. Do you have any idea where he is?"

She bit her lower lip, then said, "Benjamin, I don't have a clue, and that's the truth. It's your job to handle this situation; you know that, don't you?"

My frustration was starting to bubble to the surface. "I'm trying to, but I need to talk to him if I'm going to figure out if there's any truth to this claim. Earnest looked too smug about mentioning him to be lying. I've got a feeling there's more to this than a bluff, even if the surveyor is on his payroll."

Mom faltered, then said, "If you want to know where Paulus is, you'll have to ask your sister."

My mother hated to admit that she didn't know everything that was going on with the family, so it was a startling admission coming from her. "Which sister? I could go hoarse talking to all three of them."

She shook her head. "You only need one. You know how close Paulus and Kate are. If anyone in the family knows where your grandfather is, it's going to be Kate."

I should have known that without asking. Though parents and grandparents weren't supposed to show favoritism, there had been a bond between the two of them nearly from the start. "Then I need to talk to her right now."

"She'll be here soon. Come inside, Benjamin. We need to plan our course of action." So now she was stepping in? Mom could deal with the entire mess if she wanted to, but there was something I had to do first. "You go on. I'll be in later."

"What do you have to do that's more important than this?" she asked as she gestured to the fence.

"I'm going to stand over there and keep everybody else from wrecking into it."

She wanted to fight me on it—I could see it in her eyes—but with my mother, family came first above all else, though I wasn't sure she'd apply that particular philosophy to her father-in-law. Reluctantly, she admitted, "That's smart. I'll talk with you as soon as everyone gets here."

Mom walked toward the front of the shop and I moved in the opposite direction, heading back to the truncated parking lot in back.

It took some doing—Jim nearly drove me down before I could stop him—but I finally managed to redirect most of my siblings to the alternate lot. None of them were happy about the fence, but when I told them Mom was inside waiting for them, no one lingered.

Finally, Kate was the only one who hadn't shown up yet.

I was about ready to give up on her when I was surprised to see my three brothers—Jeff, Jim, and Bob—come out of the shop together, and from their expressions of anger, it appeared that the other Perkins men were spoiling for a fight.

TWO

∘ ∘ ∘

BEFORE I could ask them what they were up to, Jim said, "We're not about to let him get away with this. Are you coming with us, Ben?"

"What exactly are you planning to do?" I had a pretty good idea what they were up to, but I had to buy some time so I could calm them down.

Known for his blunt demeanor, I knew Jim wouldn't soften his response. "We're going to lynch Earnest Joy. Come on, it's going to be fun. It's long past due, if you ask me."

"And if his son's around, we're going to string him up too for good measure," Bob added. That was a surprise, coming from the mellowest member of our family.

"Do you have anything to add?" I asked Jeff.

He grinned as he shrugged. "Not a word. I'm just here for the excitement."

I held them back as they started for Earnest Joy's shop. "Guys, we need to be careful here."

Jim tried to shove past me as he said, "Earnest Joy should have thought of that before he trespassed on our land and put that fence up."

"That's the thing," I explained to them. "He might be on the level. I saw a survey map that showed the new property lines and it looked pretty official."

"It's a lie," Jim said simply.

I'd wanted to keep our grandfather out of it, but there was no way I could do that now. I didn't want to see my brothers compound our problem, which was bad enough without any help from them. "Paulus might be mixed up in this," I said. "There's more to it than we know right now. Why don't we wait until we have all the facts before we do anything we might regret?"

There were protests and denials, but I spoke loud enough to override all of them. "Now why don't you all go inside so I can find out what's going on." There was still some grumbling, so I added, "If it turns out that a lynch mob is what we need, I'll bring the rope myself, and that's a promise."

That finally won them over. They were walking back to the shop together—and I was finally breathing again—when Kate drove up.

She did the same thing I had, pulling in and nearly tearing the fence down before managing to stop.

She got out of her car and asked, "Ben, what's that all about?"

"That's what I'm trying to find out. Where have you been?"

She looked surprised by my question. "I'm sorry I'm late, but Jacob's got the flu. I've been babying my husband half the night." She pointed to the fence. "Do you mind telling me how that got there?"

"I'd like to, but I'm still trying to figure it all out myself. Do you happen to know where our grandfather is?"

Kate frowned. "What does he have to do with this? He's trying to stay out of sight right now because of the feud he's got going on with Mom."

"Are you actually taking sides between them?" I asked. I thought Kate was too smart to get trapped in that particular snare.

She raised her palms outward. "No way. I'm just trying to keep them from killing each other until they can both calm down and see reason."

I started to lean against the fence, then hesitated as I began to wonder if Earnest might have electrified it, though I'd touched it earlier without getting shocked. Knowing him, it was a distinct possibility that he was watching me from the shadows of his building, waiting for me to touch it again before turning on the power. "Earnest Joy claims this is legitimate, and that Paulus has something to do with it. Kate, I really need to talk to him. It's important."

Instead of telling me where he was, she said, "I'll tell you what I can do. I'll call him as soon as I get inside and then I'll have him call you right back."

I couldn't believe somebody in my family was trying to thwart me when all I wanted to do was fix this mess we were in. "Just give me the number, Kate. He'll talk to me."

She wasn't about to budge, though. "If he'd wanted you to have it, he would have given it to you instead of me. Now where should I park?"

I knew better than to try to argue this particular sister out of the telephone number. "We're all in customer parking for now," I said.

Kate frowned. "I bet Mom's just loving that. I'll call him as soon as I get inside, Ben. I promise."

I followed her progress as she drove around the building and met her at the front door by the time she parked. Surveying the lot, it appeared that Where There's Soap was doing a booming business. Unfortunately, with so many of the spots taken, it didn't leave a lot of room for our real clientele.

MOM was already addressing that when I walked inside. She had the family clustered together in front of the shop by the cash register, and from the expressions on my brothers and sisters' faces, they were as unhappy about that fence as I was. Or maybe our mother's directives were bothering them.

As I took my place among them, she said, "There are no excuses and there will be no exceptions. Kate will follow each of you home, then bring you back here."

Jim said, "Why does she get to keep her car when we all have to give ours up?"

Mom wagged a finger at him. "Because she's the only one besides me who's sensible enough to drive a vehicle most of the family can fit into. I can't see everyone piling into Ben's Miata, can you?"

I spoke up, despite the heat of my mother's glare. "Kate can't do it."

There was silence among my siblings as I felt their stares bore into me. "What did you say?" Mom asked in a lowered voice she reserved for warpaths and national disasters.

I quickly explained, "If you want me to take care of that fence, and I know you do, I need Kate's help." I didn't have to say another word. Mom dug into her purse and found her keys. As she tossed them to Jim, she said, "Here's the new plan. James, you drive my minivan and follow your brothers and sisters home."

He looked smug hearing the order until she added, "When you get back, Bob can follow you home."

"So how are we all going to get out of here tonight?" Louisa asked. "Mom, this isn't going to be very practical."

"That's why Benjamin is going to take care of it as soon as possible. Isn't that right?"

I wasn't about to make a promise I couldn't keep, certainly not with all of the witnesses gathered there. "I'll do what I can. Kate, let's go make that call."

As the others left—grumbling, but not loud enough to draw our mother's wrath—I followed Kate to our break room, a place where we kept our personal items, ate, and generally hung out away from our customers. It was a small room between the boutique and the production line, and Mom kept it stocked with a better selection of treats than most bakeries had. I thought the Krankles' bakery in Fiddler's Gap might give her a run for her money, but I wasn't going to mention that to her.

I never would have found the bakery if it hadn't been for Kelly Sheer. Kelly and I had been trying to date lately— mostly unsuccessfully—due to her daughter Annie's protests. We were going to challenge that at the Fair on the Square the next day, escorting Annie together to the rides, booths, and food stands set up downtown. I was looking forward to finally getting another chance to see Kelly when Kate's words brought me back to reality.

"Stop daydreaming, Ben. We need to call Grandpa."

Trying not to look guilty about being caught, I said, "I was just trying to figure this mess out."

My sister wasn't buying it, though. "Then why were you

smiling? I know what you were thinking about. Or should I say who?"

I pointed to her purse. "Are you going to get that number or do I have to search your bag myself?"

She offered it to me. "Go ahead and try it. Watch out for the mousetrap, though. I like to keep a few surprises handy for anybody crazy enough to stick a finger inside."

"No thanks," I said as I refused her purse. Knowing Kate, she probably really had booby-trapped the thing.

"Coward," she said as she dug into the bag. As I watched her pull out an eclectic assortment of gadgets, makeup, and notes of all shapes and sizes, I marveled that she could find anything in there. In less than thirty seconds though, she held a piece of paper triumphantly in the air.

"I knew right where it was," she said.

"I didn't doubt you for an instant." I handed her my cell phone and said, "Call him, Kate."

"Let's go to your office," she said. "I need some privacy."

I couldn't believe my sister. "If you don't want me eavesdropping, I'll go out on the porch."

Kate said softly, "It's not you I'm worried about," as she pointed to the door.

Though our mother was feuding with Paulus, I knew she was dying to find out where he'd gone. That's when I noticed that the door was open a crack. Was that my mother's ear framed there? Louder than I needed to, I said, "Okay, you're right. Let's go upstairs. You'll be more comfortable in my office."

I gave my mother time to scamper away from the door, then opened it to find her pretending to read the morning paper. If it had been in her hands right-side-up I would have had a better chance of believing her ruse.

Without a word to our mother, Kate and I walked back

to the assembly line—past the idle equipment—and up the stairs. The top floor of our building housed three offices in its space and covered just the production area and storage in back. Each office on the second floor featured a large window that looked down on the sales area below, no doubt so that we could see what was going on while we were isolated upstairs. The door to my mother's office was open— as it always was, since she spent most of her time downstairs—and Grandpa's was firmly shut. He rarely used his office space since he'd scaled back his participation in the business. I had the last office in line. Unfortunately, I spent way too much of my time locked in there trying to straighten out another mess.

I ushered Kate inside, then stepped out into the narrow hallway so she could have some privacy. While I waited for her to call our grandfather, I walked down to his office. I wasn't snooping, not really, but I couldn't help wondering if there might be something there that would help me figure out what was going on. I opened the door and started to turn the light on, but then I realized that Mom would be able to see it from the sales floor below. That was one conversation I didn't want to have, so I managed with the light coming in from the window and the open door. I knew Paulus liked to keep things neat, but it was even sparser than it had been the last time I'd been in there. The desk was now clear of any sign of occupancy, and even the photos he'd kept on display were gone. I pulled one drawer partially out of his desk, and then another. Instead of the papers I'd expected to see, there was a lone telephone book in one of the drawers, and it was three years out of date. His file cabinets were empty, too. It was as if he'd left with no plans of ever coming back. Was something going on here I didn't know about? I was just walking out of his office when Kate approached me.

"Ben, I can't believe you're snooping on our own grandfather."

I frowned. "There would have to be something in there before I could snoop. Kate, what's going on?"

She looked puzzled by the question. "What do you mean?"

"That place has been cleaned out. There's nothing left."

She peeked inside. "That can't be true." After a second, she added, "Ben, there's lots of things in there."

"I'm not talking about furniture or file cabinets," I said. "Unless you count an old phone book, the place has been absolutely gutted."

She didn't believe me, or maybe she just didn't want to. After Kate had systematically opened and closed every drawer and cabinet, her frown deepened. "I don't understand this."

"There's one sure way to find out. Call Paulus back and ask him what's going on," I said.

Kate looked uncomfortable. "I'd love to, believe me, but there's a problem with that."

"What's wrong? Is he too busy on one of his larks to help us out here?" Sometimes it felt like our grandfather was reverting to his childhood, denying any responsibility for anything and just focusing on having a good time.

Kate scrunched her lips together and ran a hand through her chestnut hair before she finally answered. "The place he was staying doesn't know what happened to him. They haven't seen him in three days."

"You've got to be kidding me," I said. "They actually told you he was missing?"

Kate admitted reluctantly, "No, but the woman I spoke to commented that his bed hadn't been slept in, and she was getting worried about him."

Maybe it was more serious than one of his larks after all. "Kate, this has gone on long enough. Tell me where he is. I need to make sure he's all right."

She looked torn as she asked, "Ben, what if it's nothing? He'll be furious with me for giving him away, and you know how that man can hold a grudge."

I took my sister's shoulders in my hands. "Listen to me, Kate. He could be in serious trouble. It's time to stop this hide-and-seek game. Now tell me where he is."

Kate battled with it—I could tell by the expressions shifting on her face—until finally she said, "He's in Sassafras Ridge."

That was less than half an hour from Harper's Landing. Why would he stay somewhere that close when he had a perfectly nice house just thirty miles away? "What's he up to, Kate?"

"I swear, that's all I know," she said. The poor girl looked like she was ready to burst into tears at any second. I put my arm around her. "Kate, it's going to be all right."

"Do you honestly think so? What if something's happened to him? Ben, I'm worried."

I could have told her the truth, that I was every bit as concerned as she was, but that wouldn't solve anything.

"Let's not borrow trouble until we find out exactly what's going on. I'll just drive over there and see what's happening. What's the name of the place where he's staying?"

"The Beverly Inn on Crestmont," she admitted. "Ben, you've got to find him."

"I'll do my best. In the meantime, I wouldn't say anything about this to anybody else in the family." She knew as well as I did that I'd meant our mother.

"I won't, but hurry, would you?"

If anything had happened to Paulus, chances are it had already occurred, but I didn't say that. "I'm on my way."

As I raced out the door, Mom tried to stop me. "Benjamin, where are you going?"

I wasn't about to share my suspicions with her. "I'm doing what you asked me to do, trying to clear this mess up," I said as I hurried out. Glancing at her as I left, I could see the concern on her face as well. She knew something was wrong, but she also knew better than to push me for more of an answer than I could give her.

I got into my Miata and drove as quickly as I dared toward Sassafras Ridge. It was time to see what had happened to Paulus, and at the moment, that was even more important than the fence cutting off our lifeline.

WHEN I got to the Beverly Inn—a place I'd never heard of before in my life—I began to wonder even more about my grandfather's state of mind. I'd been expecting a cheap dive given Paulus's penurious nature, but instead, I found a grand home converted into a bed and breakfast. The magnificent old Victorian had been freshly painted, with lavender gingerbread trim glowing against a purple field. A pristine white sign was positioned near the cobblestone walk that led past a lush lawn to the wide front porch. I might even stay there myself someday, if I ever won the lottery. One night's visit was probably as expensive as a month of rent for my apartment.

There was a Shaker-style desk in the front parlor, with a Queen Anne table beside it. The welcoming space was decorated with an eclectic selection of antiques that somehow all seemed to fit.

No one was around, and I didn't see a bell, so I called out, "Hello? Is anyone here?"

A young woman with frazzled blonde hair came out, her apron covered with flour. "I'm sorry, but we're full right now," she said.

"I'm not here about a room. You just talked with my sister about one of your guests: Paulus Perkins."

She looked flustered by the admission. "My husband told me I shouldn't have said anything to her. I'm afraid he was quite displeased. There was no need for you to rush over here. I'm sure he's fine. Jeff certainly believes so."

"My grandfather's probably fine, but I'd still like to see his room," I said.

She looked startled by the request. "I'm afraid I can't do that. Our rooms are private."

I wasn't about to let that stop me. "I'm Paulus's grandson. Understandably, the entire family is worried about him. If I could just have a look around, maybe I could clear this all up."

She nodded and was pulling a ring of keys from her apron pocket when a tall, muscular man with a crew cut came out to join us. "Mary, aren't you going to finish the biscuits?" He caught sight of me and said, "Hello. Sorry, but you've caught us at a bad time. If you'd like to book a room, you might try later today."

"I'm here about my grandfather," I said. "Paulus Perkins."

He scowled at his wife a second, then said, "Sorry, we can't help you."

Jeff tried to back me down with his glare, but I wasn't about to give up that easily. I repeated my request. "I need to see his room."

He stared at me another full ten seconds, then said, "No way. We don't allow that. Good-bye." Then he dismissed me and turned to his wife. "Mary, you need to finish those biscuits. Our guests are going to be down soon."

"He has a right to be concerned, Jeff," she said softly. I wanted to cheer—I was so proud of her for standing up to him—but I didn't want her to take any of the heat that was meant for me.

I said, "If you insist on doing this the hard way, I can be back here with the sheriff in ten minutes. Your other guests might not like it, though."

Jeff forgot all about his wife and took two steps toward me. I thought for a minute he was going to take a swing at me, and I braced myself for it. Instead, he stopped two inches from my nose and said, "I doubt Billy's going to back you up. Best friends have a way of watching out for each other."

Great. If we had been in Harper's Landing, I could have had Molly over there in a heartbeat. As it was, this oaf had called my bluff. Well, one thing I knew about poker was that if somebody called your bluff, one viable option was to go over the top and up the stakes even more, trying to force them to drop out of the hand. In a voice much louder than I normally used, I said, "That's great. We can make it a party. The health inspector for the county happens to be my cousin. I'm sure he'd be interested in looking around your kitchen." I didn't have any such relative, but I was hoping he would believe that I did.

A few guests started down the stairs and must have heard my threat. It was all I could do not to smile as they started back to their rooms. Jeff's face reddened, and I was ready to duck his punches any second. The man really should sign up for some anger management classes, but I didn't think it was the right time to suggest them to him.

"Leave before I throw you out," he snarled. Mary had ducked back into the kitchen, and I couldn't blame her a bit. I wasn't about to give up, though.

"Give me five minutes in his room and I won't bother you again," I said. "He's checking out, and I'm taking his luggage with me." He smiled coldly at that, though I didn't know why.

I added, "If you've got a problem with that, I suggest you call my attorney." I handed him one of Kelly's cards, knowing she'd back me up. "Why make this any harder than it has to be?"

I wasn't sure if he wanted the fight or not, but I think Kelly's card was enough to finally convince him I was a gnat he couldn't afford to swat. "Fine," he said as he stormed upstairs. How in the world did this man run a business dealing with the public on such an intimate level? I didn't care how elegant the surroundings, or even how nice his wife seemed. He was an oaf and a bully, and I couldn't wait to get away from him.

He unlocked the door to the Elderberry Suite and said, "Happy? You've got five minutes."

I stepped inside, then called out, "Hang on a second. You made a mistake."

"What are you talking about?" he asked as he came into the room.

"This one's empty," I said.

"That's what my wife told you," he replied, starting to leave again.

I wasn't finished, though. "Then where's his luggage? That bed hasn't been slept in, and there's nothing of his here."

"It's pretty clear, isn't it? The old man is gone, but he forgot to tell anybody he was leaving." He tapped his wristwatch. "You've got five minutes. When you're through, I'll have his bill ready and we can settle up at the front desk."

He slammed the door behind him. I searched the room, but if Paulus had left anything behind, I couldn't find it. There was a notepad by the telephone, but it was blank as far as I could tell. I checked all of the pages anyway, but there was nothing there. Or was there? I held the top sheet to the lamp and studied the heavy impressions on it. My grandfather had a firm hand when he wrote, and I knew in the past he'd torn a letter or two signing his name with such force. Grabbing a pencil from the table, I lightly brushed the sheet with its edge, hoping to leave a graphite trail. There was a telephone number there, faint but unmistakable. I dialed the number, but there was no answer. I had hoped that when the machine picked up, I'd at least be able to tell who I was calling, but an electronically generated voice invited me to leave a message, which I chose not to do. I scribbled the number down and tucked the paper in my pocket, swept through the room one last time, then left to go downstairs.

Jeff was waiting for me there, a bill in his hands. "We take cash, checks, or credit cards," he said as he pushed the invoice into my hands. I looked at the total and couldn't believe it. There were six nights of charges there, close to a thousand dollars altogether. I shoved the bill back into his chest. "I'm not paying that."

"Then I'll see you in court. Bring your fancy lawyer with you; we've dealt with deadbeats before."

I protested, "Your wife told me herself that he hasn't even been here the past three days."

The big man shrugged. "He didn't check out, and I couldn't rent the room until he did, so you owe me the money."

"Give me a second," I said as I took out my cell phone and called my mother. She was the one in charge of our finances, and if I charged something that she didn't approve, I knew full well she'd dock me for it and take it out of my salary.

When I got her on the line, I said, "We've got a situation I need your help with," I said.

"What did you find out? Can he put that fence there?"

I'd forgotten all about the blockade. "I'm still not sure. This is about Paulus. He's been staying in a bed and breakfast in Sassafras Ridge, but they haven't seen him in three days."

There was a short pause, then she asked, "Do you think something's happened to him?"

"That's what I'm trying to find out. In the meantime," I added, lowering my voice, "they want me to pay his bill. It's nearly a grand for six days' stay."

"So pay it," she said abruptly.

"What? You can't be serious. The woman who runs the place admitted to me that he hasn't even been here for three days. This is extortion." I couldn't believe my mother was folding to the pressure so easily when she fought for every dime when it came to our bottom line.

"Your grandfather's a big boy," she said. "Pay the bill. If he has a problem with it, he can dispute it himself. Otherwise, I'll pull it out of his partners' account." She sounded almost gleeful about the prospect.

"Are you sure this is the best way to handle it?" The last thing I wanted was to get in the middle of another dispute between my mother and grandfather.

"Think of it this way, Ben. We're doing him a favor. Who knows how much longer they would have tried to soak him if you hadn't stepped in? Just do it."

I reluctantly agreed, then asked, "Aren't you the least bit worried about Paulus?" I knew the two of them had had their share of troubles over the years, but there had to be a glimmer of mutual respect between them. I'd seen it myself occasionally in the past.

"Of course I am," she said. "After all, we need to know exactly what Earnest Joy is talking about. So you'll find your grandfather and get him to tell you. Now I've got to go. We've got a delivery truck, and no way to unload it."

I hung up and saw that Jeff had been eavesdropping on my conversation.

"I'll pay you for three days," I said, not willing to give him the satisfaction of winning without a fight.

"You'll pay for the entire stay, or I'll see you in court. Believe me, you won't win."

Well, at least I'd be able to tell Paulus I'd tried. I could barely stomach it as I handed him my business credit card and said, "I want a signed receipt for payment in full."

"Of course," he said as he ran it through his system. I signed the slip, had him sign the more formal bill he'd thrust at me before, then walked away. The encounter had left me with a bad taste in my mouth, but at least I had one lead to follow up on.

THREE

. . .

IT took me ten minutes, but I finally got Molly Wilkes on the phone. She was my onetime girlfriend and sometimes date, as well as being the best cop on the Harper's Landing police force. Things had been a little dicey between us since I'd started going out with Kelly, but I was hoping our friendship could transcend the momentary riff between us.

"Hey, Molly. It's Ben."

"What do you want?" she asked curtly. Okay, maybe this wasn't going to be as easy as I'd hoped.

"I need a favor," I admitted.

She sighed into the receiver, then said, "Ben, I'm not sure I should help you, even if I can."

"Hey, it's nothing, really. I just need to find an address for a telephone number."

She snapped, "It's something, believe me. Ben, I can't just drop everything I'm doing whenever you get into trouble. Go to the library and find a reverse directory. It's not that hard."

"If I can find it at the library anyway, why won't you help me?"

Her sigh was one I was all too familiar with. "Because you're asking me to do something during my shift that can't possibly be part of my job description. I have to answer for my time, you know."

"Don't you even want to know what this is about?" I asked. I had some serious fence-mending to do with Molly, more than I'd realized, but I couldn't imagine that she'd just turn her back on me.

"Fine, go ahead and tell me. What is it about?" she asked in a tired voice.

"My grandfather's missing, and this number is the only lead I've got."

That certainly got her attention. Molly and my grandfather were friends, something I'd never really fully understood. He'd called me a fool on more than one occasion for not marrying her, and threatened to ask her himself if I was too stubborn to do it.

Molly said, "I'm listening. Tell me what happened."

After I brought her up to date, she asked, "Why didn't you call me about the fence? I thought I'd be first person on your list. Well, second, anyway."

It was pretty obvious she meant Kelly was probably first. "I haven't told anyone outside the family," I said. "I've been trying to find Paulus first, because he might have an idea about what's going on."

She hesitated, then said, "This may take a few minutes. Are you on your cell phone?"

"Yeah, but I thought you just had to punch a few numbers into your computer. I don't mind holding."

She let out a snort. "Benjamin Perkins, believe it or not,

I've got more important things to do than drop everything to take care of you."

"Sorry," I said, but she'd already hung up on me. I sat out in front of the B&B in my Miata waiting for her to call back. After three minutes, I saw the front door open and Jeff came outside. He had a baseball bat in his hand, and I decided I could just as easily wait somewhere else. As I drove away, I offered a smile and a wave, but he didn't return either.

I parked in front of an abandoned movie theatre and waited there. The view was a lot less inspired, but it felt friendlier staring at the tattered posters in the displays out front than an angry innkeeper.

Molly finally called back ten minutes later. "Take this down," she said, then read me the address.

"Thanks," I said, hoping to get it in before she could hang up on me.

To my surprise, she actually stayed on the line long enough to say, "I'm doing this for Paulus. Let me know what you find out."

"I'll do that," I said as we were disconnected.

The address Molly gave me was in Sassafras Ridge, but I didn't have a clue how to find it. I'd located the inn by driving into town and searching street signs as I went, but I hadn't seen a Sunbeam Lane in my travels. I was certain that was a name I would have remembered. After driving around pointlessly for ten minutes, I spotted a post office, parked in front, then walked inside. They'd have to know where Sunbeam Lane was if the occupant there ever got any mail.

There was an attractive young woman working a crossword puzzle at the desk behind the counter. She smiled at me as I walked in and asked, "May I help you?"

"I'm looking for Sunbeam Lane," I said.

She laughed, a sound I enjoyed from the second I heard it. "Can you believe some of our street names around here? We've got Brightside Avenue, Happy Boulevard, and Rainbow Street. The man who laid out our streets was either an eternal optimist or barely sober. I haven't been able to find out which, and to be honest with you, I'm not sure I want to know."

"Is it far from here?" I asked.

"No, just drive two blocks down Happy, make a right on Sunshine, and you'll see Sunbeam on your left, two streets down the road. If you get lost, I'll be here till five."

"Thanks," I said as I headed back to the Miata. I hoped this wasn't a dead end. I needed to talk to Paulus, and it just wasn't to be sure he was all right, though I was concerned enough about his well-being. That fence was already killing our business, and it was up to me to find out how to get rid of it. Unfortunately, I had to talk to my grandfather before I could figure out where to start.

BINGO! Paulus's car was parked in the driveway of the house on Sunbeam Lane. I didn't have a clue what he was doing there, but I was starting to feel much better about him being missing in action. The small house was in need of a coat of paint and the front yard hadn't been mowed in a month. I walked up and knocked on the front door after searching in vain for a doorbell.

An older woman dressed in a bathrobe with her hair in rollers answered the door. "Yes?"

"I'm looking for Paulus Perkins," I said.

She studied me through a single misplaced false eyelash. "There's nobody here by that name," she said as she tried to close the door in my face.

I put my foot inside, willing to take the chance that she wouldn't try to break it. "That's his car in the driveway, and I found your telephone number on the night table of his room. I'd like to speak to him, please. There's no use denying you know him."

"I didn't say I didn't know him," she snapped. "I just said he wasn't here. He's not, either." She glanced at Paulus's car, then looked back at me. "Did you drive that thing back here? I thought he took it with him."

"I'm in my Miata," I said as I gestured to my car parked on the street. "If he's not here, then where is he?"

She looked me up and down, then said, "You're a persistent fellow, aren't you?"

"When it comes to family I am. Now are you going to go get him, or do I have to come back with a cop?" Hey, I didn't say it would be a police officer in Sassafras Ridge, though I'd probably have better luck with one here in town than anybody in Molly's office at the moment.

"He's at the diner down the block," she admitted reluctantly. "It's called the Lazy Spoon."

I didn't believe her, though. "Then why is his car in your driveway?"

"How should I know? Maybe he felt like a walk. Who knows what that man gets into his head. Now excuse me, but I'm not nearly ready yet, and I'm late for work as it is."

I hastily pulled my foot out of the door before she could slam it. What in the world was my grandfather doing with this woman? It seemed like every time I found an answer to one of my questions, it just confused me more than ever. I'd seen a diner on the drive in, but I wasn't about to walk there. Paulus might have all the time in the world, but I was working under a deadline.

Sure enough, I found him having a cup of coffee when I walked into the Lazy Spoon. It wasn't the most glamorous of names, but then I wasn't planning on eating anything there, so what did I care?

I slid onto the bench seat beside him and said, "You're a hard man to track down."

He nearly choked on his coffee when he saw me. I was about to call the paramedics when he waved a hand in the air. "I'm all right. You just caught me off guard. Don't you know any better than to sneak up on an old man like that?"

I shook my head. "If you'd let one of us know where you were, I wouldn't have to."

He shook his head in clear disgust. "I figured it was too much of a coincidence having you walk in here like that. I can't believe Kate ratted me out. I never would have believed it."

"Don't blame her. I practically had to force it out of her, and she still wouldn't have told me anything if there hadn't been an emergency."

That certainly got his attention. "What happened? Is something wrong with your mother?"

"There's something wrong with all of us," I said. "But before we get into that, I want to know what you think you're doing."

He started to get up. "I won't sit here and listen to your scolding. I changed your diapers, or have you forgotten that?"

Leave it to Paulus to bring that up. I sincerely doubted he'd ever gotten within half a mile of a dirty diaper in his life, but there was no one willing to dispute his claim that he'd changed me and each of my siblings once and only once. Knowing him, it was probably true. Paulus was the kind of man to do something like that just so he could bring it up twenty or thirty years later.

It was time to smack him right back. In a piercing voice, I said, "You're still a part of our family and our business, or have you forgotten that?"

That got him. For just a second, Paulus looked every bit of his seventy-plus years. After a few moments, he settled back into his seat and said sadly, "If that's true, then why don't I feel like I am?"

I couldn't believe he'd have the nerve to say that. "Remember, I argued with you not to leave when Dad died until I ran out of breath. I needed you, Paulus, and you just dumped Dad's job right on me. It was just about more than I could take."

Was that a tear forming in his left eye? Whatever it was, he brushed it away before it had the chance to hit his cheek. "When James died, a part of me died with him. I couldn't stand being around the shop anymore." He looked steadily at me as he added, "Besides, it was your place to step in, not mine. You're the future of Where There's Soap, Ben. I'm the past."

That explained a lot. I'd always thought my grandfather had downsized his role to advertising as a way to retire without officially quitting. Instead, it appeared that he'd mostly left our business because he'd had to get away from the memories it held for him.

"We're both the present, Grandpa," I said. I almost always called him Paulus, and the use of that honorific got his attention. He stared down into his coffee for a few seconds, then said, "Maybe I was a little hasty then, but you're doing a fine job now."

I hadn't come looking for praise, no matter how welcome it was. "So what are you doing on Sunbeam Lane? Is that your new girlfriend?"

I wasn't sure what reaction I'd been expecting, but I certainly hadn't thought what I said was all that amusing. After he managed to get his breath back from laughing so hard, he said, "Boy, you know me better than that. Lois and I have been friends for donkey years, but I wouldn't date her if she was a piece of carbon."

That still didn't answer my question. "So why did you leave the Beverly Inn three days ago and move in with her?"

His voice rose. "Blast it all, I'm not cohabitating with that woman, I just dropped in to say hello. I'm staying out at the Moonbeam Motel on the highway. It's fifty bucks a night, but I don't have to eat there, so that's a bonus."

I shook my head in amazement. "I can't believe you've been paying for two rooms and just using one."

He frowned. "What are you talking about?"

"You forgot to check out of the Beverly. I put your bill on the company credit card, but Mom says you have to pay it back. It was close to a thousand dollars."

That time he did jump out of his seat. As he stood over me, he said, "Why did you pay him? I told that scoundrel I was leaving after the second night, but he claimed I'd made the reservation for six days, and then said I had to pay for every bit of it. Now we'll never get our money back."

"It's not our money, it's yours," I corrected him, knowing that Mom's fiscal policy was in concrete. "So why did you check in there in the first place?"

He looked sheepish as he admitted, "I misunderstood the price. It turned out forty-five dollars was for lunch, not the whole room. I found out on the third morning of my stay, packed my bags and left. The wife seemed nice enough, but that man's a menace."

"And he claimed you made a reservation for six nights," I said.

"You saw the place didn't you? I couldn't pass up that kind of deal, so I booked it for six days the second I saw that room."

I shrugged. "So dispute the bill. I put it on a credit card. I wouldn't advise going back there without an armed guard. When I left, he was coming out on the porch with a baseball bat. Now will you stop blustering and sit down? I still don't know what you're doing in Sassafras Ridge."

Paulus looked around us, saw that no one was listening, then said, "There's a business opportunity I'm looking into, but if it's just the same to you, I won't say anything else about it just yet."

"You've already got a job," I reminded him.

"Maybe I'm in the market for something different," he said. "No offense, but lately that family of yours has been a little oppressive."

It was my turn to laugh. "Just a little oppressive? You're kidding, right? Besides, they're your family, too."

"You know what I mean. Sometimes I just have to get away, and I thought something else here might hold my interest."

At least I finally knew what he'd been up to, though I'd noted how careful he'd been to skirt the real issue of what he was doing in town.

"I've got something for you, if you're bored," I said. "Earnest Joy put a fence up last night across our back parking lot. When I asked him about it, he told me to talk to you."

Paulus wasn't the least bit surprised by my news, something that deeply disturbed me. Instead of the rant I'd expected, he said softly, "So it's come to that, has it?"

"You mean that land really does belong to him?"

"It's complicated," Paulus said. He slid a single under his plate, then grabbed the bill. "Come on, we need to get back to Harper's Landing."

"That's what I've been saying all along," I said.

As he headed for the register up front, he added, "We're going to need some help dealing with this. Have you called Kelly Sheer yet?"

"No, I wanted to talk to you first," I admitted.

My grandfather snorted in disgust. "What are waiting for, Ben? As soon as you drop me off at my car, give her a call. You can't waste another second. I'm afraid we're going to need her services on this one."

I was afraid of that too, given Paulus's serious demeanor.

"Kelly, we've got a problem," I said as soon as I dropped Paulus off at his car. I knew I probably should have called Kate and Mom first about Paulus, but I didn't want to delay getting Kelly involved for another second.

"Are you cancelling our meeting at the Fair on the Square?" she asked. Was that hope in her voice, or was it just my imagination? "It's okay if you have to. I'll understand."

"No, I wouldn't miss that for the world. I'm talking about the soap shop. I'm afraid we need your legal expertise again."

"What is it?" she asked.

I explained the fencing problem to her, and after I was finished, she said, "Let me get one of my assistants to research the title at the courthouse. I'll let you know by five. Listen Ben, I've got to go."

She hung up before I could even say good-bye. Something was definitely up with Kelly. I had to wonder if her daughter Annie was giving her a hard time about our date the next day. She was just eleven and hopelessly in love with the idea that her parents would someday get back together, and I didn't fit into her plans at all.

I dialed the shop's number, hoping that Mom wouldn't answer. No such luck.

"I found him," I said.

"Where was he, shacked up with some trollop?" she asked. Man, was I ever glad I hadn't called in after meeting Lois and jumping to the wrong conclusion.

"No, he's looking into some business opportunities."

"Soap business?" my mother asked coolly.

"No, actually it's none of our business at all," I answered.

She took that in, and I could tell she wanted to dispute my response, but finally she said, "I'm assuming he's all right, so that's what's important. Did he shed any light on Earnest Joy's claim?"

"I couldn't get much out of him," I admitted. "But he said we needed to call Kelly. I'm not at all sure that means the news is good, are you?"

Mom hesitated, then said, "Benjamin, I honestly thought you would have called her first. Haven't you at least talked to her about the situation?"

"Of course I have," I protested, not admitting the exact time I'd called her. "She's looking into it."

"And you need to as well, Benjamin. This has to take priority over everything else. Don't worry, I'll have Cindy teach your class this afternoon."

My youngest sibling had agreed only recently to teach, but she had requested a few more training sessions under my tutelage before she took over alone. I'd planned to help her during my hand-milling class later that day, since it was a process I loved to teach. "She can observe, but it's my class," I said.

"Son, I know how important teaching is to you, but it's vital you fix this fence problem immediately."

I wasn't about to back down. "I've got good people on it, Mother. I'm teaching the class. As soon as I'm finished, I'll get right back to it, but this is important to me, too."

Her sigh was clearly audible. "Fine, teach away."

"I will," I said as I hung up. I could have gotten Louisa or Kate to teach for me—they were both good at it—but I enjoyed my classes, and I loved keeping my hand in soap-making, even as an instructor. It wasn't just a vocation for me, it was an avocation.

When I got back to Where There's Soap, I was pleased to see that the parking lot was full, and only one of the cars belonged to the Perkins clan. When I walked in, there was a healthy crowd inside, and I recognized some of my students from past classes. I ducked back into the classroom to prepare for the day's lesson when Kate joined me.

"Thanks again for pointing me in the right direction," I said as I retrieved the hand graters out of a box and set some of them out on the five tables of the classroom. It was a nice space, with room for supplies and materials, microwaves and hot plates for melting soap, and plenty of room to work.

"Was he mad at me?" Kate asked.

I grinned. "He wasn't all that happy with you until I told him I had to practically torture you to get the information. I kind of think he was proud of you for holding out as long as you did."

The relief on my sister's face was obvious. "Thanks for that."

"Hey, it's the truth." As I started lining up some of the oils, fragrances, and other additives we'd be using, I added, "Is Cindy around? She's helping me with this class today."

Kate nodded. "She's coming in a second. In fact, I'm to give you express orders not to start without her. What did you say to her to get her to change her mind about teaching?"

I shrugged. "I guess it's just part of my charm."

Kate frowned. "There's got to be more to it than that."

I threw a clean dish towel at her. "Thanks for your vote of confidence. You've delivered your message. You can go now."

She tossed the towel right back at me. "Oh, there's one more thing. There's somebody out front who's been asking about you."

I glanced at the clock and said, "I don't have time to talk right now. I'll have to speak to them later."

"Believe me when I tell you that you'll want to see this visitor before she gets away. She's tall, a brunette, and prettier than you have any right to expect. Believe it or not, she seems to be very interested in my big brother. You're still dating Kelly, aren't you?"

"As far as I know." I had to admit, Kate had intrigued me.

I started for the door, and she said, "Hey, I thought you had a class to teach."

"I do, but I can't be rude to our customers, now can I? Would you mind finishing the setup for me?"

She grinned at me as I walked out of the classroom. "I guess I could, since you're dealing with a customer."

"Wipe that smirk off your face," I said with a smile of my own. Who in the world could be visiting the soap shop and looking for me? It didn't take long to find out. Waiting just outside the classroom door was a tall, curvaceous woman I instantly recognized.

"Diana? What are you doing here?" Diana Long owned and operated a mystery bookstore in town called Dying To

Read. I'd had some dealings with her in the past, and we'd gotten along from the start. Her long brown hair was always pulled away from her face, showing off her big brown eyes.

"Hi, Ben. You talked so much about this place the last time you were in the bookstore that I had to come see for myself." There was a twinkle in her deep brown eyes that made her appear to always be up to something, and a smile just waiting for an excuse to burst out.

"And you trusted the place to Rufus?" The young man in question was her assistant manager and head clerk, a college student with an inordinate fondness for murder and mayhem.

"Are you kidding me? He's constantly complaining that I'm never gone from the bookstore. I think he's been planning a coup from the first day I hired him. He's in absolute heaven."

Cindy came toward us, tapping her watch as we made eye contact, then walked into the classroom. I said, "Listen, I don't mean to be rude—I'm thrilled you came by—but I've got a class to teach."

She nodded. "I know, I'm signed up for it. In for a penny, in for a pound."

"Excellent," I said. "If you'll excuse me, I've got some last-minute prep work to do. I'll see you inside."

"I'll be there," she said.

When I walked back into the classroom, Kate and Cindy were standing there waiting for me.

"We're not sure we approve," Kate said.

Cindy added, "She seems nice enough, but we were under the impression you were dating Kelly."

Kate shot back, "And you know how we feel about men who date more than one woman at a time."

"Slow down," I said. "Diana and I aren't dating. She

runs Dying To Read, and I happened to mention the soap shop the last time I was there."

Kate shook her head. "She's not here for the soap, big brother."

"Maybe the soapmaker," Cindy added with a grin.

"Enough, you two. I've got a class to prepare for."

Kate pointed to the front. "Everything's ready. We've got loads of time to talk more about this."

I glanced at the clock and saw that we were two minutes away from beginning. "I've got a great idea. Why don't we start early today?"

"Chicken," Kate said.

I pretended to study my class list. "Funny, I don't see your name here."

She smiled at me as she left, and Cindy said, "We were just teasing."

"I know. You do realize I'm interested in Kelly, and just Kelly, don't you?"

Cindy hugged me. "Ben, everybody in the world knows that. That's why we've been teasing you. Do you honestly think we'd be that cruel if you weren't? Okay, don't answer that."

I ignored her as I opened the door and announced, "For those of you registered for our soapmaking class, it begins in two minutes."

Diana was the first one inside, taking a seat by my desk. Was there any truth to my sisters' teasing? I certainly found her attractive enough, and we'd hit it off from the start. Maybe if Kelly wasn't in the picture, I conceded. But she was, so I dismissed the speculation and watched as the others came inside. Two people on my list, names I was well familiar with, weren't there yet, but I waited as long as I could, then started to close the door.

"Hang on," a voice I knew called out.

"We're coming," the other said.

Herbert and Constance Wilson, two of my more interesting students from the past, rushed to the door, both nearly out of breath.

"You're late," I said with a grin.

Herbert said, "I was ready an hour ago. She couldn't decide on what to wear."

"Herbert Wilson, that's not fair and you know it. My first outfit would have been fine if you hadn't spilled root beer all over it."

"You joggled my arm, woman. It wasn't my fault. Besides, no one would have noticed. You were wearing your brown pantsuit."

"I would have known," Constance replied.

I knew from experience that this could go on for hours, and I had a class to teach. "If you two are ready, let's go in so we can get started."

The older couple walked inside and scanned the room. Before they could say anything, I said, "You'll have to sit back here. Hope you don't mind."

They took a seat at one of the back tables, and I heard Constance say, "If you hadn't been so clumsy, we would have gotten our spots from before."

"Be quiet, woman, the man's trying to teach."

It was a bit of a blessing that the Wilsons were sitting in the back. Maybe I'd miss Herbert's whispered critiques of my lessons, but I doubted it.

"Welcome," I said as I stood at the small teacher's table in front of the room. The five long tables were nearly full, and I marveled yet again how many people in our community had embraced soapmaking. The walls of the classroom were lined with shelves containing everything from abrasives to volatiles, and four microwave ovens were anchored in each of the room's corners. We used the microwaves instead of stovetops for much of our melting, but we also had hot plates we'd need today. Cindy stood in back where she could get a good view of my lesson.

"Today we'll be learning one of the basic methods of soapmaking. It's called hand-milling or rebatching, and some of the finest soaps in the world are created with this method. Hand-milled soaps have a finer texture than other soaps, and they last longer, too." I held up one of the standard generic white bars of soap and said, "This is our first building block in creating an individualized and unique soap. Don't think of this bar as a finished product, because it's just a beginning ingredient." I put the soap down, then held a container of dye up in one hand and a baggie filled with oatmeal in the other. "For one of our first soaps, we'll be using some simple additives, but it's amazing what you can come up with once you learn the basics of this process. There's a combination that will do just about anything you want, if you just know the right ingredients to add."

"I want to look forty years younger," an older woman in back tittered.

"You'd have to be wrapped up in a baby blanket if you did," I said, and the class laughed right along with the two of us. "Seriously though, there are soaps that reduce stress, increase energy, help insomnia, and even ones that actually clean your hands."

"What about noodles?" Constance asked from the back of the room.

"Someone's been studying," I said, and she smiled. "We'll be using soap noodles in our next class," I told everyone, "so we'll go over them then."

"But what are they?" an older man asked.

I called out, "Cindy, would you mind grabbing a few bags and passing them around? Class, this is my sister Cindy, and one of the best scent-makers to walk this planet."

My sister shot me a cold look as the classroom pivoted in their chairs to get a look at her. She had no other choice but to retrieve a few bags of the soap noodles and pass them out. As the class looked at them, I explained, "These noodles are extruded from the same formula as our basic bar of soap. While it's true they are easier to work with since the hand-milling step is skipped, I think it's important to build your first soap from the beginning of the process. There's a history in hand-milling soap that goes back hundreds of years. Cindy, would you mind passing out the soap bars so we can begin? I'll distribute the trays while you do that."

My sister came forward and started doing as I asked. I offered her a smile and said, "Thanks." As I passed out trays to catch the shavings of the white base soap to each student, I noticed that Diana was watching me. Well, I *was* the teacher. Why shouldn't she watch me? Blast my sisters for planting the thought in my head that she might be interested in me.

"Use your graters and reduce the soap I gave you," I told them. "It's just like grating cheese." As they worked the soap down to shreds, I said, "Watch those knuckles. We don't want any impurities in our finished products."

After everyone had a neat pile of soap shavings on the trays in front of them, I said, "Now is where the fun begins. For today, we're all going to make the same type of soap together to learn the process. Tomorrow we'll be using soap noodles," as I said that, I nodded in Constance's direction. "Then in our final class we'll be experimenting with individual soap blends. Now it's time to gather the tools and ingredients we'll need for today's session." I'd thought about handing everything out at the same time, but I wanted them to get a feel for the soap on their hands before we complicated the procedure. As I moved from station to station on the long countertop, I distributed measuring bowls, wooden spoons, hot plates, pots, and other equipment. Once those were passed out, I gave each of them premeasured containers of water, dye, and fragrance. Finally, I handed out small bags of oatmeal and molds I'd made from sections of plumbing pipe that were perfect for our needs.

"Put the soap you've grated in your glass measuring containers, then add the water I gave you. Next, place the container into the pan and turn your hot plates on."

"Why not use the microwaves?" Herbert asked.

"We could," I admitted, "But for the first time, I like you to be able to see the soap actually melt and coalesce. That's tough to watch in a microwave." I wasn't a big fan of using microwave ovens for soapmaking, though some of my sisters actually preferred them. I personally liked to watch the shredded soap and water combine slowly, a dance that delighted when it transformed into a silky base ready to enhance.

As everyone waited for the water in their saucepans to boil, I gave them my talk on the history of soap. It filled the time nicely, and I thought it was important for them to realize they were participating in a process that was thousands of years old. I noticed most of them were ready, so I said, "When you achieve a fairly smooth consistency, lower the temperature to a simmer, and then stir the soap occasionally. Don't worry if it looks a little lumpy right now. We're just trying to get everything melted. Stirring helps, but do it gently. If you stir too hard, you'll get suds, and we don't want them right now."

After another minute, Herbert said, "This looks more like cottage cheese than soap."

"Then you're doing it right. Keep stirring."

A little while later, Diana said, "Mine's stringy. Should it be that way?"

"That's perfect. Take the bowl out of the water and turn your hot plate off." She did as I asked, as did most of the others. "As your soap reaches this stage, you've got to work quickly. Add the dye, then put the fragrance in. Next comes the oatmeal, then stir it all in. Once you're happy with the blend, spoon what you've got into your mold. Tap the side of it a few times as you go along to get rid of the air bubbles, and you're finished."

I had to help a few students out, but Diana had done a perfect job, as had many of the others.

When they were finished, a woman named Betty from a front table asked, "Can we take these with us this afternoon?"

Ordinarily I liked to send my students home with their soap, but I didn't have enough freezer space to hurry the setting process. "No, these won't be ready for four or five hours. There's a piece of tape on each mold. Write your name on it, and you can pick your soap up on Monday."

There were a few grumbles, and I regretted once again that I'd let Mom schedule the first class on a Friday. She'd had to bump the session when she had a chance to teach a special class earlier in the week, one that profited the shop considerably.

"They'll be here for you all on Monday. Have a good weekend," I said.

With the class over, I said, "Cindy will be standing by

the door handing out some of our basic hand-milled soap recipes. Each of you should take a sheet and consider what type of soap you'd like to make during our final session on Tuesday. Thanks everyone, you all did a great job."

They didn't clap, but everyone looked well pleased with the session. Diana approached me after class was over and said, "That was a lot of fun. I'm so glad I could come."

"I'm happy you could, too."

There was a line of people waiting to speak to me, so she excused herself. Somehow Constance had beaten most of the others to me, although she'd been in the back of the classroom. "Ben, there's something I want to ask you about. I tried to do a pour last week like you taught in that other class, but it didn't work out right."

"Did you bring it with you?" I asked.

"No, I didn't think to do that," she admitted.

Saved! "Why don't you bring it early on Monday and I'll take a look at it."

She wasn't going to budge, though. "I can describe what happened to it."

Herbert touched her arm. "Let's go, Connie, I'm hungry."

"I told you not to call me Connie," she said.

"And I told you not to let me go hungry. I figure we're even."

As they headed for the door—still arguing—I answered the rest of the questions. Cindy came up front with the extra soap handouts after everyone else was gone. "That was dirty, big brother."

"If I'd answered her question, she'd never have left," I said.

"You know perfectly well I'm talking about dragging me into your class. I wasn't supposed to do anything, remember?"

I couldn't believe it. "Cindy, I just asked you to help hand a few things out. You've got to get over this fear of teaching. This isn't junior high school. These people are here because they want to learn. With the possible exception of Herbert, nobody's here who doesn't want to be. Okay?"

"I guess so," she said reluctantly. "Do you need help cleaning up?"

"No, I've got it," I said. In all honesty, straightening up after one of my classes was a nice, quiet time for me.

I was just starting to rinse the graters when Mom hurried into the classroom.

"Let one of the girls handle that," she said. "You've got a job to do."

"This will just take a second," I said, resentful that she'd intruded on my time.

"Well, I don't think Andrew Joy's going to wait for you much longer. He wants to talk about the fence."

FOUR

• • •

ANDREW Joy was studying a display Cindy had created for the shop showing which essential oils and fragrances achieved a particular result. Andrew was a squat little man with a head of thinning blonde hair, though I knew he was just in his late twenties. To overcompensate, Andrew had grown a thick, luxurious mustache that edged down his chin.

Before I could even say hello, he turned toward me and said, "Do you people actually believe this bunk? How can a bar of soap alter your mood?"

"I don't know, how can jewelry make you feel better?" I countered.

"We never claimed it did," he said. I'd been hoping Andrew was there on a peacekeeping mission, but it was pretty obvious from his tone of voice and demeanor that he was asking for a fight.

"What can I do for you, Andrew?" I asked curtly.

He actually smiled. "Good, we can dispense with the

niceties. I want you to leave my family alone." He tried to poke me in the chest with his right index finger, but I easily stepped out of his reach.

I laughed, which only made him angrier.

"What's so funny, Perkins?"

"You put a fence up blocking access to our shop and you expect me to back off? You're kidding, right? I've got a team of lawyers digging into it right now." Well, maybe not a real team, but I knew Kelly was better than anybody the Joy clan could throw against her.

"Dad was well within our rights. That land belongs to us," he said petulantly.

I was tired of dancing around these people. "According to what fairy tale?" I asked as I stepped up to him. I was a good four inches taller than Andrew, and I wanted to use every bit of it to back him down.

He took a slight step back. "We've got proof, don't worry about that."

"If you're so certain, why don't you show us? If you want us to leave you all alone, give us a reason to."

Andrew snorted. "You'd love that, wouldn't you? There's no way we're going to give you a chance to steal our proof. An IOU from a poker game is legal, and you know it."

"What are you babbling about?"

Andrew's smile cracked his face again. "You mean he hasn't told you? I thought you'd have talked to Paulus by now. Honestly, Ben, I'm beginning to believe you're not nearly as smart as everyone in Harper's Landing thinks you are."

He started to leave, but I wasn't finished with him yet. I grabbed his arm, and he jerked it away violently.

"So now you're going to try to beat me up, is that it? I'll sue you for assault and battery. You've lost your mind. You and your entire family are lunatics. You should all be locked up."

That was all I could take. There was no way I was going to stand in my own shop and have the man insult me and my family. I grabbed his arm harder this time and started walking him toward the front door. He tried to struggle, but I forced him outside. I hated that my class saw my behavior, and no doubt some of them would drop out because of it, but I wasn't in the mood to worry about the ramifications of my actions at that particular moment.

Once I had him outside, I nearly shoved him off the porch. "Go home, Andrew."

When he was fifteen feet away, he said, "I've got witnesses! You'll be sorry you did that." As he rubbed his arm, he said, "When I get back to town on Monday, I'm swearing out a warrant on you."

"Why wait?" I said. "Let's go downtown right now." The adrenaline was starting to wear off, but I still wasn't sorry for what I'd done.

He shook his head. "I'm late right now for an appointment in Raleigh. Monday will be soon enough for you to go to jail."

He scampered back toward Joy land, and I had to fight the urge to follow him, just to see what he'd do.

Mom walked out onto the porch, and before she could say anything, I admitted, "Okay, maybe I shouldn't have thrown him out like that, but he had it coming."

To my surprise, my mother just smiled at me. "I came out here to tell you how proud I am of you. No one should be allowed to insult your family, Benjamin."

I wasn't sure if I was happy with the praise or not. As for the threat of arrest, that didn't bother me too much either. I'd worry about it when and if the time came later.

The last thing I wanted to do was to go back inside the soap shop, but I didn't have much choice. I wasn't sure what the reaction would be, but I never expected applause. When I walked through the door, my brothers and sisters were lined up near the register clapping.

Bob said, "Way to go, man. We heard you yelling from the production line."

Jeff added, "You really let him have it."

Louisa looked at me and said, "Don't let him get to you, Ben. He always was a little weasel."

"Guys," I said, "I hate to ruin the party, but there's a very good chance that I may have just made things worse."

Mom said loudly, "Enough. We have these wonderful customers still to wait on, and gentlemen, you have a specialty production run to finish. Now back to work, everyone."

I wanted to hide in my office, but Diana caught me before I could get upstairs. "I'm sorry to hear about your troubles."

"We'll work it out," I said. "I'm the one who should apologize. I let him get to me."

She touched my arm lightly. "Ben, there's nothing wrong with defending your family. I think you did exactly what you should have done."

"Thanks," I said, then I noticed that Kate and Cindy were watching us. "Well, I've got a mound of paperwork waiting for me upstairs. If you'll excuse me."

She took the hint instantly. "Absolutely. I need to get back to the bookstore. It's hard to tell what Rufus has done in my absence. I'll see you Monday, Ben."

"See you then," I said.

I retreated up the stairs to my office, hoping to get away

from the world for a while. There was a knock on my door not ten seconds after I'd closed it.

"Go away," I said.

The door opened and I saw Louisa standing there. "Now is that any way to talk to your favorite sister?"

I grinned at her. "Who said you were my favorite?"

"Why wouldn't I be?" she asked with a smile of her own. "Now why don't you take me to lunch? You haven't eaten yet, have you?"

I looked at the clock and realized that I'd missed another meal. Sometimes my schedule was so busy I literally forgot to eat. It was probably a good thing, though. With the baked goods Mom kept on hand downstairs, I could stand to skip a meal every now and then. "I'm not all that hungry," I said just as my stomach growled loudly.

"What was that, coyotes? Come on, let's go to The Hound Dog. I'm in the mood for one of Ruby's sloppy burgers."

"Why not," I said as I stood up. "I'm not going to be able to get much work done anyway. Andrew's a real jerk, isn't he?"

"Like father, like son. We'll detour the Joy property and go the back way, what do you say?"

I grabbed my jacket. "I say let's go."

We walked to The Hound Dog, chatting aimlessly about anything that crossed our minds, except for fences and neighbors. By the time we walked in to Elvis Presley's voice serenading us with the grill's name and inspiration, I felt much better. Though I loved all my siblings equally, there was no denying the special bond between Louisa and me.

Ruby, the owner of the diner, was dancing when we walked in, but didn't look the least bit self-conscious when she saw us. "Grab a booth or a spot at the counter, I'll be with you in a second."

We found a booth away from the jukebox, and as soon as the song was finished, Ruby joined us. I'd been studying the vast array of Elvis memorabilia on the walls. I could swear some of it was new, though where she'd found the room to display anything else was beyond me.

Ruby handed us a pair of menus and said, "You two are eating a late lunch, aren't you?"

I smiled. "How do you know we're not having an early dinner?"

She laughed. "You're right, I don't. What can I get for you?"

Louisa ordered her burger and a diet soda. "I'll have the same," I said. "But make mine an iced tea."

"Coming up," Ruby said.

Once she was gone, Louisa looked at me steadily, then said, "So tell me about your love life."

Oh no. Was that why she'd wanted to have lunch? I would have rather discussed the Joy men than talk about what was going on in my personal life.

"You go first," I said, hoping that would dissuade her from the topic.

To my surprise, she said, "I'm still dating John Labott, and you know it."

John was one of our suppliers, and he'd had a crush on Louisa forever, but he had always been too shy to do anything about it. It had finally gotten so bad that Louisa had asked him out herself.

"How is that going?"

Louisa shrugged as Ruby delivered our drinks. "When it comes to love, you never know, do you?"

Ruby said, "Amen to that. Just listen to the King."

I waited until she was gone before I said softly, "She thinks Elvis has the answer to everything."

"Who knows? Maybe she's right. Enough about me, though. What's going on with Kelly?"

"I'm not sure. Listen, do you really want to hear this, or are you just making polite conversation?"

Louisa took a sip of her soda. "Ben, have you ever known me to be polite about anything? I really want to know."

"Okay, here goes then. We're supposed to take her daughter Annie to the Fair on the Square tomorrow, but to be honest with you, Kelly doesn't seem all that excited about it. I'm beginning to wonder if she's having second thoughts. Honestly, I'm thinking about cancelling myself just to save her the trouble."

"Benjamin Perkins, that is exactly the wrong thing to do. Honestly, do you know anything at all about women?"

I held up my hands. "Hey, take it easy on me. So what do you think I should do?"

"I think you should go ahead with your plans. If Kelly wants to cancel, she will. You know how strong-willed she is."

I took a sip of tea, then said, "That's one of the reasons I'm so fond of her."

"Then give her some time, and trust her judgment. If she's having second thoughts about anything, she'll tell you."

I thought about it, and realized that Louisa was probably right. Kelly was a strong, independent, and assertive woman. Until I heard otherwise, I was going to keep our date for the next day. I was saved from any other discussion by the arrival of our burgers, and it was nearly impossible to talk while eating one. After we were finished, I was glad for the chance to walk back to Where There's Soap. At that point, any exercise I could get was worthwhile.

I hesitated when I got to the porch, and Louisa asked, "Aren't you coming in?"

"No, I'd better do a little more checking on this fence. I want to pin Paulus down and see if Andrew knows what he's talking about."

"See you later, then." I started for the Miata when Louisa called out, "And Ben, don't worry about Kelly. Things will work out."

"I hope you're right," I said. Mom had given me special dispensation to park with the customers on the grounds that I was trying to get the situation resolved, and I'd need my own transportation to do it.

I drove to Paulus's house, but his car was gone and no one answered the doorbell. Where in the world could he be? I thought about calling Kate and asking her, but even if she knew, I wasn't sure she'd tell me. I'd pushed her once, but I didn't think I'd have a chance pushing her again so soon.

As I drove around town trying to think of anything I could do to help the situation, I suddenly found myself parked in front of Kelly Sheer's law office. Now how had that happened? Was I there to check on her progress on our case, or was it for more personal reasons? Either way I had a legitimate reason to visit her, and if I could get a better read on our situation while I was there, that was fine, too.

Kelly's office was in a complex downtown near the courthouse, the main professional building for Harper's Landing. There were three other attorneys in the building, along with two accounting firms. I walked into her office and saw that she'd hired a new receptionist. The man was in his late twenties, and I hated to admit it, but he was quite a bit better looking than I was.

"May I help you?" he asked before the door could close behind me.

"I need to see Kelly," I said.

"Do you have an appointment?" he asked as he scowled at his computer terminal.

"No, but she'll see me if she's here."

He gave me a look that conveyed how sorry he was, and how deluded I must be. "She's in conference at the moment, then she's due in court. If you'd like to make an appointment, I'd be happy to set you up with something late next week."

"Tell her Ben Perkins is here to see her," I said, fighting the urge to blow past him and tell her that myself.

If he recognized my name, he didn't show it. "Mr. Perkins, I'm afraid I can't interrupt her at the moment. She's . . ."

Kelly came out of her office. Her long blonde hair was pulled back, and wire-rim glasses were perched on her nose. She looked great in her tailored suit, but I preferred her in blue jeans.

"Ben, what are you doing here?" I'd had warmer welcomes from people I had to collect money from.

"I need to talk to you," I said.

"I tried to tell him you were busy," the receptionist said.

Kelly took my arm and pulled me into an empty office, no doubt where a partner would be someday. "What's this about?"

"What did you find out about our property line?" I asked.

She frowned. "It's not as simple as I thought it was. There's some doubt about the original survey. I'll have to look into it myself on Monday."

There was no way in the world I could wait until then. "Why not now? This is important, Kelly."

"And you don't think what I'm doing is? I'm in a meeting at the moment, and then I've got to be in court. By the time I'm finished, the register of deeds will be closed. I'm sorry, but I've got to get back in there."

"That's fine," I said. "I didn't mean to interrupt."

A handsome man about my age poked his head out of her office. "Kelly, is everything all right?"

"It's fine," she said curtly. "I'll be right there."

The man looked at me like I was unworthy to be taking up space. I was getting a great many more hostile reactions than I'd been expecting when I'd decided to visit Kelly.

He finally closed the door, and I said, "There's no short-age of good-looking men around here, is there?"

Kelly sighed. "Ben, I really do have to go."

"Sorry to keep you," I said. I knew she had a practice to run, and that I couldn't expect her to drop everything to help me. I could hope, but I couldn't reasonably be angry if she didn't.

As she ducked back into her office, I asked, "We're still on for tomorrow aren't we?"

"I'll be there," she said.

So that idea had been a complete wash. I tried to think of anything else I could do, but Paulus was AWOL again, Kelly didn't have time to help, and Andrew and his father were both being stubborn mules. I'd thought Earnest Joy had been the truculent one, but Andrew had been more adamant about that fence than his father had been. So should I try to talk sense into Earnest? The poker debt that Andrew had mentioned sounded bogus to me, but I'd have to hear Paulus's side of things before I acted.

I was pulling out of the parking space in front of Kelly's office when I noticed my grandfather's car parked in front of Myra's Shoes. I pulled back in and shut off the engine. It was time to talk to Paulus about what was really going on.

He was trying on a pair of pristine white walking shoes when I found him inside. "There you are," I said. "We need to talk."

I swear, it looked like he wanted to run away. I just wasn't having much luck with my people skills, even with my family.

"What about?" he asked grumpily.

"A poker debt. Does that ring any bells?"

Paulus looked at Myra a second, then said, "Do you have these in elevens?"

The slim older woman with bright white hair said, "Paulus, I told you before, they're not going to fit."

"Humor an old man, would you?"

She shook her head as she said, "I swear crusty old geezers like you will be the death of me someday."

After she ducked into the storeroom, we had the place to ourselves. Paulus leaned toward me and said, "So you know."

"Know what, that you bet our back parking lot in a game of poker and lost?"

He rubbed his chin, then looked me in the eye. "Ben, it was a long time ago. I was drinking then, pretty heavily, I might add."

This was the first time I'd heard about it. "How bad was it?"

"I blacked out a few times," he admitted. "I don't remember the bet, or even the poker game, but Earnest showed me the note the next day, and my signature was on it. We were friends up until then, but that ended that. He never said another word, and I just figured he tore the chit up and threw it away. I never dreamed he'd actually try to collect on it. I'm sorry."

Paulus looked as if he wanted to cry, and I put an arm around his shoulder. "Listen, we'll work this out, okay?"

"I know you're the family fix-it man. If you can make this right, I'll be eternally in your debt, and I mean it."

I stood. "I'll do what I can. And thanks for coming clean with me."

"What are you going to do now?" he asked.

"I'm going to go see Earnest Joy."

Paulus looked like he'd rather take a beating, but he offered, "Would you like me to go with you?"

"No, I'd better handle this alone." As I left the store and drove toward Earnest Joy's house, I finally felt like I was doing something productive. From the hours I'd seen posted at his store, I knew he would most likely be home. I wasn't going to threaten or bully the man—I knew neither approach would work—but I was going to tell him we were fighting it all the way.

Earnest's Cadillac was parked in front of his house, so I knew he was there. The Joy family homestead was an older place. I knew Earnest could afford a much better home, but he's stayed in the place he'd grown up. There had to be something sentimental about the man to want to do that. If I could find that part of him and appeal to it, I might not have to sue.

I couldn't see a doorbell, so I knocked on the front door. It yielded to my touch and swung silently open. "Earnest?" I called out. "Are you there?"

There wasn't a sound from inside, and I thought about just leaving. After all, he might shoot me and claim I was breaking in, knowing how ornery the man could be.

I'd just turned to leave when I saw flashing lights behind me. Molly Wilkes jumped out of her squad car with her gun drawn. I instantly put my hands up in the air. True, this was the same curvy brunette I'd taken to the Senior Prom,

but it was also an officer of the law drawing a bead on me.
"Hey, it's just me."

"What are you doing here?" she asked as she approached.

"I'd feel a lot better if you'd put that gun down," I said.

She shook her head. "Not happening. We just got a tip
that something bad happened here. Don't follow me in. I'll
be back in a minute."

I knew better than to try to argue with her. I waited
while she entered the house, her gun sweeping an arc as
she entered. There was nobody I'd rather have looking out
for me than Molly. She was smart and competent, and I'd
heard from more than one source that she was the best cop
in Harper's Landing.

I must have held my breath the entire time she was inside. Six minutes later I heard an ambulance approach, and
two men with a gurney rushed inside. I wanted to follow
them in, but Molly had been pretty clear about my instruc-
tions. She came out a minute later and gave me a look I
hoped I never saw again in my life.

"Tell me what happened," she said in a flat, official
voice.

"What's going on?" I asked. "Is somebody hurt?"

She stared at me a few seconds, then said, "Actually,
somebody's dead."

"What happened?" I asked. A thousand scenarios raced
through my mind, none of them good for me and my family, given the current state of discord between the Perkinses
and the Joys.

"I'm asking the questions right now. Ben, I'm just going
to ask you one more time. What went on in there?"

"Molly, I swear I don't know what you're talking about.
I just got here two seconds before you showed up. There's

no bell, so I knocked on the door. It swung open, so I started to go inside, and then I saw your lights. That's all that happened."

She shook her head. "Did you touch anything while you were inside?" she asked.

"No, not a thing."

"Then you're staying out here until we can process the scene."

Another car drove up, and a man I didn't recognize got out. He spoke to Molly briefly, and then walked inside.

"Who's that?"

I could see in her eyes that she wasn't sure she wanted to tell me, but finally she admitted, "That's the new coroner. We can't move the body until he gives us his approval." A woman outfitted with kits and cameras came up in a police van as she spoke and went in, too.

"I can't believe Earnest is dead."

She snapped, "What makes you think it was Earnest? I didn't say anything about who it was, and to be honest with you, I was kind of surprised you didn't ask when I came back out."

"Come on, Molly, it's his house. Who else could it be?" Then I remembered my pretty public fight with Andrew three hours earlier. "Oh no. It's not Andrew, is it?"

"Ben, I knew you all were battling about that fence. Does this have anything to do with that?"

I said loudly, "How would I know? You won't even tell me who it is."

"You were right the first time. It's Earnest Joy. And there's a problem."

"Just one?" I snapped. "I can't imagine what it could be."

"You might want to save the theatrics for someone

who's impressed," she said. "It's pretty important you keep it all in check right now."

I took a few deep breaths, then said, "I'm sorry. So what's the problem?"

"I shouldn't be telling you this, but it's pretty clear that Earnest was murdered. The worst part of it is that he's got a bar of soap from your shop clutched in his left hand."

That news shook me more than the murder. "Molly, you can't honestly believe that I had anything to do with this. You've known me practically my whole life."

She didn't answer immediately, a fact that shook me to the core. When Molly finally spoke, she said sadly, "I don't want to believe it, Ben, but I know how you can be when your family is involved. All of you Perkinses are extremely protective of each other."

"Not to the point of murder," I said hotly.

"And then there's your temper. You can fly off the handle sometimes, and you know it. So give me an alibi or something else I can believe. It might help once we determine the cause of death."

I thought about my whereabouts for the past few hours. While it was true that I'd spent some time with people who could verify where I'd been, I'd also driven around alone, certainly long enough to sneak over to Earnest Joy's house and bash in his head.

"I can't account for every minute of the last few hours," I admitted. "Molly, even if I did kill him, would I have been stupid enough to leave a bar of soap in his hand? Come on, that doesn't make sense."

She shook her head. "I wish it were that simple, but from the blood and the way he was positioned, it was pretty obvious that Earnest grabbed that soap after he was attacked. It was still in its wrapper, Ben; that's how we knew where it was from."

"Wait a second," I said. "His son Andrew was in our shop three hours ago. He could have bought some then, or slipped a bar into his pocket."

"We'll talk to Andrew as soon as we can find him," Molly said. "Do you happen to know where he or Terri are?"

I thought about my earlier confrontation with Andrew. "I don't know where Terri is, but Andrew's in Raleigh by now. He left right after our argument."

Molly shook her head. "Don't tell me. You two were fighting about that stupid fence."

"It's going to kill our business if it's true that the Joys own that land," I said. "That makes it pretty serious."

She stared at me a second, then asked, "Ben, do you *want* me to lock you up? I don't need much more reason now than you've given me this afternoon."

"Do what you have to do," I said. "I don't care how bad it looks. Somebody else killed him."

"We'll look into Andrew's alibi and his sister Terri's too, but we're going to be talking to your family as well. I've got to tell you though, you're the most logical suspect, given the facts."

It looked like I was going to jail, despite my innocence. "Can I at least call Kelly and have her meet us at your office?" I didn't relish spending the night behind bars, but I knew on one level that Molly was right. It did look bad for me.

"Don't be a bigger horse's rear end than you already are. I'm not locking you up until I have more evidence than I've got. But do me a favor and hang around town, would you? I've got a feeling I'm going to get some heat for not taking you in right now."

I offered my thanks, then said, "I may need to go to Sassafras Ridge or Fiddler's Gap, but I won't go more than seventy miles from here without telling you first."

She shook her head. "You're all heart, aren't you?"

Ralph Haller, Earnest's crony from the shop, came charging out from the house next door. "Is it true? Did you kill him?" he asked, shouting as he hurried toward me. "You did, didn't you? You sick jerk, he had every right to put that fence up."

"Take it easy," I said. "I didn't kill anybody."

Ralph pointed to Molly with his right index finger. "You've got to arrest him. I heard him threaten Earnest yesterday."

"You're lying," I said, a little louder than I'd meant to.

"Prove it," Ralph said.

Molly stepped between us. "Sir, if you'd like to make a statement, why don't you go back and wait on your porch and I'll talk to you in a few minutes."

Ralph stared at me with a crazy glare in his eyes. "You bet your hat I want this on the record." He stared at me a second, said, "Killer," then walked back to his property.

Molly watched him go, then asked, "What was that all about?"

"He was Earnest Joy's best friend."

She shook her head. "Ben, is it true what he said?"

"I never threatened Earnest Joy," I said, trying to keep my voice level. "He's making it up."

"Did he witness any conversation at all between you and Earnest yesterday?"

I couldn't believe this. "Molly, he was at the jewelry store when I confronted Earnest about that blasted fence. I may have raised my voice once or twice, but I didn't threaten him. I swear it."

She paused, then asked, "Was anybody else there?"

I shook my head. "No, it was just the three of us."

"Great, that's just great, Ben. Nicely done. The next time you get into an argument with a man who's about to be a murder victim, could you at least have the courtesy to get a witness who doesn't want to see you go to jail?"

There wasn't much I could say to that. "Am I free to go then?" I asked.

"Where can I find you if I need you?"

I looked her straight in the eye. "Do you really want to know?"

"I wouldn't have asked if I didn't."

I took a deep breath, then said, "I'll be out looking for who really killed Earnest Joy."

She finally blew up. "Don't make this worse than it already is, Ben. You're in way over your head."

"Maybe I am," I snapped, "But at least I know I didn't kill him. Can you say as much?" I paused a few seconds, then added, "Yeah, that's what I thought."

Before Molly could say another word, I walked off. All the way to my car, I half expected her to call me back to the porch so she could arrest me, but when I didn't hear anything, I felt a sense of relief, no matter how temporary it was. While it was true that I was under pressure to figure out who had killed Earnest Joy, I didn't have a single idea where to start. Besides, there was one other thing I needed to do before I started my own investigation. I had to tell my family what had happened, and it wasn't going to be much fun adding that I was the prime suspect.

Suddenly jail didn't look so bad after all.

* * *

I parked in the customer lot of the soap shop, but before I went in, I had to call Kelly.

When her receptionist answered, I said, "Kelly Sheer, please."

"Whom may I say is calling?"

"Tell her it's Ben Perkins," I said.

There was a hint of glee in his voice as he said, "I'm sorry, Mr. Perkins, but Ms. Sheer is unavailable."

What an officious little twerp. "Just put her on."

"I'm afraid she's gone for the day. You could try back Monday morning."

"That's all right," I said, "I've got her cell phone number."

After I hung up, I dialed her cell, only to find out that it was turned off. Kelly never did that, and I wondered if she had done it just to avoid talking to me.

Don't be so paranoid, Ben, there's probably a perfectly good reason she's out of touch.

I left a brief message on her voice mail and asked her to call me. Then I added lamely that I was looking forward to tomorrow and hung up. I couldn't delay it any longer. It was time to tell the family about Earnest Joy.

At least it was close enough to closing time to lock the doors before I told them. As expected, everyone was shocked by the news of the homicide. Before I could even finish, my brother Jim said, "You were with me all afternoon, remember?" He added with a wink, "You can bet your life I'll testify to it in court, too."

Mom looked relieved by the news. "Is that true, Benjamin?"

Jim kept nodding, but I said, "No, ma'am, I can't actually account for all of my time this afternoon. I had plenty of opportunities to sneak over there and kill him if I'd wanted to."

Mom slapped Jim's hand.

As he rubbed his knuckles, he said, "Ow. What was that for?"

"For lying to your mother," she said, then she slapped him again. Though he was a grown man who towered over her, he took it, though he protested the treatment. "What did I do that time?"

"You didn't believe in your brother's innocence," she said simply.

"You've got it all wrong. I'm trying to keep him out of jail. I know he didn't do it. It's the rest of the world I'm worried about."

Mom bit her lower lip, then reached up and hugged him. "I'm sorry, Jimmy, I shouldn't have swatted you."

Bob said, "Don't be too easy on him. I'm sure he deserved it for something else."

Kate snapped, "Would you boys grow up? This is serious."

"It's worse than you realize," I said. "Molly's going to interview all of us about the murder. She's going to want to know about your alibis, because I'm pretty sure she thinks she's got the motive and the murder weapon wrapped up."

"Why that's wonderful news," Mom said, and I wondered if she'd had a little toddy with her lunch.

Louisa asked her before I could. "And why is that such good news?"

Mom looked smug as she explained. "It means that she's not a hundred percent convinced that Ben is the one who killed Earnest."

Cindy muttered, "But we're her only other suspects."

I said, "It's not just us. She's going to talk to Andrew and Terri, too."

Jeff was surprisingly quiet during the conversation. I

looked at him, but he wouldn't make eye contact with me. A sudden feeling of despair hit me. Could my brother have killed the man out of some sense of family? "Jeff, is there something you want to say to me?"

"Not me," he said, and that was all I could get out of him.

Mom shook her head, no doubt just as confused as I was, then she said, "So here's what we'll do. We're going to go about our business and let the police handle this. For now, it's going to be business as usual at Where There's Soap." Mom glanced at the clock, then said, "Right now, it's time to go home. I won't pay overtime for you all to sit around trying to solve a murder." She tossed her keys to Louisa. "It's your turn to take everyone home."

They were grumbling as they left, and I tried to follow them out when Mom called out, "Ben, may I speak with you a moment?"

Blast it all, I'd almost made a clean getaway. "What's up?"

She waited until the front door was locked and no one was left but the two of us. Then she turned to me and said, "So what are you going to do about this?"

"What are you talking about?"

Mom squinched her eyes at me. "How are you going to solve the murder so this doesn't touch us?"

"What happened to letting the police do their jobs and us doing ours?"

"That's nonsense," she said. "I said it to appease your brothers and sisters, but we both know better. We can't afford to wait for them to see the truth. You've got to figure out what really happened to Earnest Joy."

I took my mother's hands in mine and said, "Mom, I wish I knew how to manage that, honestly I do, but I'm stumped. Molly's going to talk to Andrew and Terri, the crime lab's probably still at the house, and most likely there are two or three other cops working on it. What does that leave me?"

She smiled. "You've got something they don't."

"Please, enlighten me," I said.

She tapped my forehead. "You've got this. So go home and think about it. Make a list like you always do and find an angle that Molly might miss."

I shook my head. "You give me too much credit."

"Ben, you are very good at this. Don't underestimate yourself. I don't want you to come in tomorrow. This is more important. Besides, with the Fair on the Square, we won't have many customers, if past years are any indication."

"I've kind of got something else going on tomorrow," I admitted.

"Tell me, what could be more important than this?"

I finally admitted, "I've got a date with Kelly Sheer and her daughter."

Mom smiled. "Well, I'd have to say that's at least as important as this. Go, have a good time, but don't forget, you need to keep working on this. We're all counting on you."

No pressure there, having the entire Perkins clan depending on my ability to better a trained police force. "I'll do my best. Good night, Mom."

"And to you, Benjamin."

I grabbed a pizza on the way home to my apartment and settled in for the night. Television couldn't hold my attention and neither could the three books I tried to start reading from my waiting pile. The image of Earnest Joy dying with a bar of our soap in his hand kept haunting me, and finally, barely after ten, I gave up and went to bed. I might as well have stayed up for all the rest I got.

When I finally dragged myself out of bed the next day, I

realized that not even a cold shower would bring me back my normal bouncy step. As I shaved, I realized I should be excited about my first family outing with Kelly and Annie.

So why was I dreading it?

FIVE

○ ○ ○

I waited by the old stone chimney near the Square, the rendezvous point Kelly and I had agreed on. It was close enough to the action to see everything gearing up, but still easy enough to spot each other. The petting zoo was nearby—filled with bleats and baas from the goats and sheep—and I could smell popcorn and funnel cakes in the air. I was a good half hour early for our allotted meeting time, and I fully expected to wait. That's why I was so surprised when Kelly showed up a minute after I got there. She was alone.

"Where's Annie?" I asked, trying not to believe the sad look in Kelly's eyes.

"Ben, we need to talk," she said solemnly.

I had never had a conversation with a woman in my life that started off with those particular words and didn't end in disaster.

"Go on," I said, ready for the bad news. I was half expecting it from the way she'd been acting lately, but I never could have imagined the reason why.

"Wade and I are going to try to reconcile," she told me, the blow of her words nearly staggering me backwards. "It's for Annie's sake," she added, obviously trying to soften the sting of her words.

"You can't be serious," I said. "After everything you told me about him? Is Annie enough of a reason to put yourself through that again?"

While he hadn't been exactly abusive, Kelly had told me enough about Wade to make me despise the man for the way he'd treated her.

"He's changed," she said, her voice nearly breaking. "I'm so sorry to do this to you."

The other shoe finally dropped. "Wait a second. That was him in your office yesterday, wasn't it?"

She reached for my hand, but I was in no mood for it. In a plaintive voice, Kelly said, "Don't make this any harder than it already is."

"Why shouldn't I?" I protested loud enough to draw the attention of some parents waiting for their kids at the petting zoo. That was too bad, let them listen. "Kelly, don't do this. There's something special going on between us."

"I know that," she said, barely choking out the words. "I'm not thinking about my own happiness. I'm doing this for Annie."

She left me standing alone, and there wasn't a thing in the world I could do about it.

My first reaction was to get out of there. I wasn't in the mood to be around a lot of people, most of them happy and joyous to be together.

Maybe Kelly was right. I had to grant her the possibility that Wade had changed, but even if he hadn't, Kelly had been pretty emphatic about her decision, and the reason behind it. She was doing it for her daughter, and as much as I wanted to, I couldn't fault her for that. My parents were together until my father's untimely death, and it had meant a great deal to me having them both right there whenever I needed them. If Kelly was making a sacrifice for her daughter, wasn't that what parents did? My loyalty to my own family made me realize that, even though there was the potential for a truly great love between us, she had a daughter to consider.

Even if I could change her mind, I wasn't at all sure I had the right to.

I felt an arm grab mine and looked up to see my sister Louisa standing there. "Hey, bro, what's up?" She took one look at my face and asked, "Oh, no, did someone else die?"

"Just a budding romance," I said, quickly telling her what had happened.

"Ben, I'm so sorry. Would you like to go somewhere and talk about it? I'm a great listener; you know that."

"I wouldn't dream of doing that to you." I looked around. "Hey, where's John?"

She shrugged. "He had to go to a sales conference at the beach this weekend with his company. From the way he described it, they'll talk about business for ten minutes then golf the rest of the time. So what do you want to do? I'm all yours."

I thought about leaving the Fair and taking my sister up on her offer to listen to my problems, but the last thing I wanted to do was to hold a postmortem over a relationship that barely had the chance to bloom, no matter how promising the bud had been.

"Tell you what," I said. "Why don't we check out the Fair since we're already here?"

"Are you sure? I don't mind missing it. Really I don't."

"I'm positive," I said. "After all, maybe it would do me some good."

She put an arm through mine and led me toward the festivities. "Then let's go and have some fun."

There were more than a few whispers and indirect looks my way as Louisa and I walked past the street vendors and displays. There was no doubt in my mind that news of Earnest Joy's homicide had already been rehashed over breakfast tables throughout Harper's Landing, and I was pretty sure that everyone in town knew I was the chief suspect. I didn't let it get to me, though; I tried my best to forget about what had happened with Kelly, too. It didn't work, but I still tried.

Set up in the center of the Square was a series of big glass pickle jars, the kind that restaurants must use. In front of each jar was a sign describing an item that was being raffled off for the fire department's fund-raiser. They were in dire need of a new truck, and with the budget cuts that had been hitting our state lately, this was probably the only way they were going to get it.

As Louisa veered off to buy a caramel apple, I took a closer look at the signs, then I asked the young woman with a nametag that read Sarah, "How many things are being raffled?"

She smiled as she counted the items on her list. "Believe it or not, nobody's asked me that today. We've got twenty things we're giving away, but some of them you probably won't like."

I smiled at her. "Now how do you know what I might not like?"

She grinned as she looked at me and said, "Funny, you don't seem the type to like manicures and pedicures."

"You never know if you don't try, do you? I'll take twenty tickets."

As she took my twenty-dollar bill and exchanged it for the requisite number of tickets, Sarah explained, "Put your name and phone number on each ticket, then drop them in the jars. We're drawing at five p.m. but you don't have to be present to win."

I did as she said, depositing a ticket into each jar without even looking at the prize offered. With my luck, I probably would win the manicure and pedicure. If I did, I'd give the certificate to Louisa. I didn't know how she'd managed it, but she'd found me at exactly the right time, just when I'd needed her.

My sister joined me as she took another bite of caramel apple. "She's a little young for you, isn't she?"

"What are you talking about?" I asked.

"That girl at the table. I saw you flirting with her. What is she, sixteen?"

"I wasn't flirting with her, and she's got to be older than that," I said. "I'm sure she's at least in college. Who knows, maybe she likes the older, distinguished type."

Louisa poked me. "More likely you remind her of her dear old dad. Face it, Ben, to women in their twenties, you're practically invisible."

"Hey, I'm not that old," I protested.

"Dream on, Brother."

Surprising us both, I leaned over and kissed my sister's cheek.

"What was that for?" she asked.

"For being here when I needed you. Thanks."

Louisa looked embarrassed by the display. "I didn't do anything," she protested.

"There you're wrong."

She looked at some of the rides that had been set up on the Square. "So are you up for some fun?"

"You'd have to be crazy to get on that Ferris Wheel," I said, "let alone the Spider. They put these things together in the middle of the night. What makes you so sure they didn't miss a bolt or two in the dark?"

"Come on, take a chance."

I shook my head. "You go ahead. I think I'm going to take off."

She looked longingly at the rides, then said, "Let's go then."

"No, I want you to stay and have fun. I'm going to be fine. I promise."

She didn't want to let me leave alone, but when I insisted, she finally agreed. "If you need me, just call."

"I will," I said, and then fought the crowd back to where I was parked. When I got into the Miata, I suddenly realized I had nowhere else to go. The only way I was going to get my mind off my hapless love life was by trying to figure out if there was anything I could do to help Molly figure out who had killed Earnest.

Maybe it would help take some of the sting out of Kelly's rejection if I occupied my mind with something else, something more urgent than a bruised heart. I drove back to Where There's Soap, but instead of going in, I walked around to the back where the fence stood. To my surprise, Terri Joy was standing there staring at it from the other side, her left hand testing its sturdiness.

"It's pretty ugly, isn't it?" she asked when she saw me.

"You could always take it down," I replied.

She shook her head. "I would if I could, but my brother has some kind of obsession with it now. He's claiming that he'll fight you to the end to fulfill Dad's last wish."

I lightly kicked the bottom edge with the toe of my shoe. "Why did Earnest care so much about it? If it mattered all that much, he sure took his time getting around to it."

Terri sighed. "Don't kid yourself. I'm pretty sure Andrew was behind this from the start. He was going through Dad's safe-deposit box at the bank and stumbled across the IOU. That was months ago, but then all of a sudden it became important to him to do this."

I gestured toward the gopher-hole garden. "More important than his horticulture?"

She laughed. "It's pretty hideous, isn't it? Hey, Dad was just happy Andrew found something he liked doing. We used to watch Andrew digging from Dad's office. That boy has developed a single-minded devotion to moving dirt."

"I'm kind of surprised you're even talking to me," I said. "Terri, it's important to me that you know I didn't have anything to do with what happened to your father. I lost mine, too. I know how much it hurts."

She wept without appearing to even acknowledge the tears. "I know you wouldn't hurt him, Ben."

"Thanks for believing me," I said.

Her words sharpened. "Don't think I'm letting you off the hook completely. I still think his murder had something to do with this dispute. Just because I said I don't think you did it doesn't mean I'm ready to absolve your entire family."

"Terri, I can assure you, none of my family would do something like this."

She stared at the fence a moment longer, and I wondered what she was going to say, when I heard Andrew's voice coming from the back of the jewelry shop.

"Leave her alone," he shouted as he came at a trot.

"I'm fine, Andrew," she said, turning back to look at him.

She might as well have saved her breath. As he approached us, he said, "I mean it, Perkins. I'm not going to let you bully my sister, so don't even try it. You've already murdered one member of my family, and I'm not about to let you hurt another one." He had his fists clenched, and there was a fire in his eyes. Was I going to get into a fistfight, at my age? I wasn't looking for a confrontation, but if that was what he wanted, I had a lot of anger and frustration I wouldn't mind venting out on him.

Not even trying to hide the scorn in my voice, I snapped, "I didn't kill your father. Stop being such a jerk."

Terri stared at me a second, then turned to her brother. "Honestly, you both need to grow up. Andrew, nobody's going to bully me, you know that. We don't know what happened to Dad yet, so stop jumping to conclusions."

She turned to me and added, "As for you, you're not making things any easier. You know that, don't you?"

Without another word to either one of us, she walked away. That seemed to take the steam out of the argument. Andrew followed docilely behind her. I kicked the fence out of frustration—much harder this time—but he didn't look back; he didn't even break stride.

Staring at the fence wasn't getting me anywhere, so I walked around front and came into the soap shop through the main, and at the moment, only entrance. There were a couple of customers milling about, and Cindy sat behind the register. She was reading something, but I couldn't tell what it was.

"Goofing off?" I asked her as I approached.

"Hardly," she said as she held up a book outlining different careers. "I'm trying to decide what to do with my life. Nothing all that important, just little stuff like that."

My youngest sibling was barely past eighteen, and uncertain about her future. While the rest of us had followed the Perkins tradition of working at Where There's Soap—either after high school or college—Cindy wasn't sure if she wanted to spend the rest of her life making soap.

"There's plenty of time to decide," I said.

She shook her head. "I agreed to work here for one year after high school, since all of you did the same thing, but after that, I'm just not sure."

I tapped the book. "So what are you interested in?"

She looked down at the book, then shoved it under the counter. "I'm not telling. You'll laugh."

"Are you kidding me? As long as it's not underwater basket weaving, I won't say a word."

Cindy and I had a strong bond, being the oldest and youngest of the Perkins clan.

I waited, and after some hesitation, she said, "If you breathe a word of this to anybody, I'll shave your head in your sleep."

I ran a hand through my hair. "Okay, that's a pretty creepy threat, but I promise to keep it to myself."

In a low voice, she said, "I think I want to be a biologist."

"You always were good in science, and especially chemistry. It might be a perfect match for you."

Cindy studied my face for a few seconds. "You're not mad?"

I smiled at my baby sister. "Now why in the world would I be mad about that? I've got a lot more problems to worry about right now than my littlest sister's career path."

She frowned. "Yeah, I heard about what happened with Kelly. I'm so sorry, Ben."

I shook my head. "The problems I'm talking about are that fence spread across our property and my being a suspect in Earnest Joy's murder. How in the world did you hear about what happened with Kelly so fast?"

Cindy looked guilty as she admitted, "Louisa called a few minutes ago. She wanted to spread the word through the family so no one would upset you with any questions."

"This family could teach the satellite communication industry a thing or two," I said.

"Don't be mad, Ben. We care about you, that's all."

"I know, but there are times when it can all be a little claustrophobic."

Cindy laughed. "You don't have to tell me that. Try being the baby of the family."

"No thanks. I've got enough trouble being the eldest. If you need me to help you out down here on the floor, I'll be up in my office."

She looked around at the nearly empty shop. "I think I can handle it, but if a mob shows up, I'll give you a call."

I walked through the boutique space, past the classroom and the break room, then into the production area. It was the only way to get up and down the stairs to my office, but honestly, I usually enjoyed walking through the place on my way to my desk. My brother Bob, the man who kept our ancient line running by manufacturing the parts we needed himself, was filing the cogs on an iron wheel as I walked back into the production area.

"What's going on?" I asked.

"I'm trying to make a piece fit where it wasn't meant to be, and it's giving me a major headache." As an afterthought, he added, "Sorry about Kelly."

"Yeah, me too," I said, hopefully burying the topic with him. Just four more offers of condolences from my siblings, maybe a word or two from my grandfather and a lecture from my mother, and I'd be out of the woods.

Bob stared at me a second, then said, "Do you want to talk about it?"

I laughed. "Not particularly."

His relief was pretty obvious. "Good. Jessica's been trying to get me to communicate more at home, and it's driving me nuts."

"If that's your worst problem in the world, you've got a pretty good life. How is your wife, by the way?"

He looked around, though no one was nearby. "Can you keep a secret?"

"Absolutely. What's up?"

He grinned broadly. "She's pregnant. Can you believe it? I'm going to be a dad."

I hugged him as I pounded him on the back. "That's great news," I said. "Congratulations. I bet Mom's going nuts about her first grandchild on the way."

"She doesn't know yet," Bob confessed.

A wave of dread swept over me. "So I have to keep this from her? Bob, she'll kill me when she finds out I knew before she did." My mother liked to think she was on top of everything, in our family and our business. I didn't want to be anywhere nearby when she learned that I'd scooped her on what she would consider the most important news of her life.

"Listen, you can't even let on to Jessica that you know. It was just killing me not telling someone, you know? When we announce it formally, you need to act as surprised as everyone else, okay?"

"I'll win an Oscar," I said. "Do you think I want anyone else to know that I was in on it?"

"Good. I knew I could count on you."

"So how far along is she?" I asked.

"Two and a half months. We're going to make an announcement in two weeks when the first trimester's over. I still can't believe it."

"Congratulations," I said, pounding his back again.

"What are you two celebrating?" my brother Jeff asked as he walked back to the shop.

I was about to make something up when words suddenly deserted me. Jeff was standing there with Molly Wilkes, but it was pretty obvious she wasn't at Where There's Soap investigating Earnest Joy's murder. Molly's luxurious long black hair was down and she was wearing a pretty dress, but that wasn't the first thing that caught my eye. She and Jeff had been holding hands when they'd walked in. Unless I was way off, it appeared that my baby brother and my former girlfriend were out on a date.

Molly let her hand slip from Jeff's when she saw that I'd noticed. "Hi, Ben," she said quietly.

"Molly," I replied.

Jeff looked like the biggest rooster on the farm. "So what are we celebrating?"

I thought about a lie I could come up with when Bob said, "I think I've finally got that part right."

Jeff looked at us both like we'd lost our minds. Trying to keep my voice as casual as I could, I asked, "So what are you two up to?"

I could see that Molly was searching for the right words when Jeff said, "We just went to the Fair on the Square, and now we're going out to lunch."

I looked at her and asked, "Is it really a good idea to be dating a suspect?"

She frowned. "That's not fair, Ben."

Jeff said, "I'm not on her list. I have an airtight alibi."

"Believe me, there's no such thing, little brother."

Jeff smiled. "Yes there is. I was having a late lunch with Molly when Earnest was murdered."

"Okay, maybe I was wrong," I said. "That would be hard to refute."

Jeff nodded, then said, "Hey, I've got a great idea. Why don't you call Kelly and we can make it a foursome for lunch?"

I could see that Molly didn't think any more of that idea than I did. Fortunately, I had the perfect answer. It had the added advantage of being the absolute truth. "She just broke up with me about an hour ago," I said.

Jeff's smile faltered, and Molly looked at me with a surprised expression. She said, "I'm so sorry, Ben. Are you all right?"

"I'd be lying if I said it didn't sting a little, but I'll be fine," I said.

Jeff's strut was gone as he said, "You could still go out with us. We don't mind."

The last thing I wanted to do was tag along with my little brother while he dated my ex-girlfriend, but I was saved from answering by Bob. "Sorry, but I need his help here. Why don't you two run along?"

They both nodded, and as they left, I saw Molly turn back and look at me a second before leaving.

I picked up a wrench and slammed it on the worktable after they were gone. "Can you believe that? What is he thinking?"

Bob picked the wrench up and moved it out of my reach. "Ben, you were dating Kelly, and you know how long he's had a crush on Molly. It's got nothing to do with you."

"So you knew about them?" I asked. "How long has this been going on behind my back?"

Bob shook his head. "Let me get this straight. You started going out with somebody else, but you didn't want Molly to date anyone, is that about right?"

It sounded pretty petulant when he said it, but I wasn't going to just roll over and accept it. Then I realized how childish I was being. Bob was right. I'd made it clear to Molly that I was pursuing a relationship with Kelly, so why shouldn't she date my brother?

"Maybe I'm being a bit unreasonable," I admitted.

Bob laughed. "You think?"

"It's just going to take me some time to wrap my mind around this," I admitted. "Now how can I help you?"

"You're kidding, right? No offense, Ben, but this is pretty delicate work. I need to do this by myself, okay?"

"I understand," I said. "Thanks for bailing me out."

He grinned. "That's what family is for."

I nodded, and as I walked upstairs to my office, I said, "And congratulations again."

"Thanks," he said, adding the biggest smile I'd ever seen on his face in my life.

I walked upstairs to my office and shuffled papers around on my desktop, not really accomplishing anything at all. I knew I should be focused on Earnest Joy's murder, but I couldn't keep from thinking about my little brother dating Molly. I knew he'd had a crush on her for years, but I couldn't believe she'd actually start going out with him. Then again, why not? Bob was right. I had made my feelings clear enough. But while Molly and I had enjoyed dating, it had evolved more into friendship as the spark died to an ember's glow. She'd had a tough time when I'd started dating Kelly, but she'd accepted it. Now I was going to have to do the same thing. I looked down into the store and saw an older man and woman shopping together. They were laughing and holding hands like a couple of kids. I'd been searching my entire life for what they'd apparently found. I even thought I'd discovered it a time or two, but it never seemed to work out for me.

"Enough, Benjamin," I said aloud. "No more moping about, no more pity party. You're a grown man, or at least you pretend to be. Get on with your life."

My pep talk was interrupted at the end by the intercom. It was a hands-free system that allowed us to communicate throughout the shop without bothering with the telephone receiver.

Cindy said, "I'm sorry, I didn't know anybody was there with you."

"I'm all by myself," I admitted.

"But I thought I just heard you talking to someone."

I laughed. "I was trying to cheer myself up," I admitted.

"You're so weird," Cindy said with real affection in her voice.

"Did you want to call me about that, or did you need something else, littlest sister?"

"You've got a phone call," she said.

"Who is it?" I asked as I reached for the receiver.

"It's Kelly," she said after a moment's hesitation.

I pulled my hand back. "Tell her I'm not here," I said. The last thing in the world I wanted was to talk to her.

"Sorry, I can't do that. I already admitted it. You might as well take it, Ben. It's not going to get any easier."

Blast it all, she was probably right. "Okay. Thanks."

"I'm here for you, Ben. We all are."

As the intercom cut off, I reached for the telephone. "Hello?"

"Ben, this is Kelly. We need to talk."

I tried to keep my voice level. "I thought we just did.

From the way we left things, it didn't feel like there was much left to discuss."

"It's about the message you left on my machine about you being a suspect in Earnest Joy's murder. Maybe it would be better if you found another attorney to help you out on this."

I couldn't believe what I was hearing. "Boy, when you bail out on somebody, you do it all the way, don't you?"

"That's not fair," she said, and I could hear a tremor in her voice.

"You're telling me. Kelly, did I do something to make you hate me?"

"What?" she asked, obviously startled. "No. Of course not."

"Then don't treat me this way. You've explained your decision, and while I don't like it for a second, I respect it and I promise I won't pursue you romantically. But I don't think Harry McCallister is up for this. I'm hoping it doesn't come to it, but if I need an attorney, I want to be able to count on you." McCallister handled our corporate stuff, but he hadn't been inside a courtroom in donkey years. "So what do you say?"

She sighed, then said, "You're right. My decision to reconcile with Wade wasn't because of anything you did. If you need me, at least as your attorney, I'll do my best to help." There was a long pause, and I wondered if she was still there when she added, "Ben, I handled this badly. I'm so sorry."

"It's your life," I said, this time unable to keep the hurt out of my voice. "I'll call you if Molly decides to arrest me. Good-bye."

"Bye," she said softly as I hung up.

And that was that. I'd had high hopes for my budding

relationship with Kelly, but they were ashes in my mouth now. We'd only shared a few dates stolen from the time she spent with her daughter, Annie, but I'd grown fond of her and would miss having her in my life. It was time to move on.

I worked at the stack of papers on my desk, going through order forms and invoices, trying to catch up on some of the paperwork I'd let slide lately. All in all it was pretty mindless stuff, but it helped to keep busy, and I didn't exactly have anywhere else I needed to be. By the time Cindy knocked on my door several hours later, I'd managed to clear my desktop, something I hadn't been able to do in ages.

She walked in, glanced down at the pristine surface, then said, "Wow, so there's real wood under there after all."

I shrugged. "To be honest with you, I'd forgotten that myself. What can I do for you?"

"We're closed," she said as she gestured to my window overlooking the store below. Nearly all of the lights were off and the aisles were deserted.

"I lost all track of time."

Cindy said, "So get up and let's get out of here. What would you like to do tonight? I'm up for anything."

"Don't you have a date?" I asked her. Cindy had a very active social life, rarely dating the same young man two nights in a row. I didn't believe for one second she didn't have plans for a Saturday night.

"It's nothing I can't put off," she said. "I'm ready if you are."

I shook my head. "I'm not about to let you break some

guy's heart for my sake. I appreciate the offer, but go out and have fun."

"Reggie won't mind, I promise. I'm here for you, Ben."

I laughed. "Reggie will probably be up on the roof if you cancel on him, ready to throw himself off. I mean it. Go on."

She frowned. "Are you sure?"

"I'm positive. I'm going to grab a hamburger on the way home and watch an old movie. That's the best thing in the world for me right now."

"I like hamburgers," Cindy said, "and if you let me pick the movie, I'll hang out with you."

"No thanks," I said. "Honestly, I need some time alone."

She reluctantly agreed. "Okay, but if you change your mind, call me on my cell phone and I'll be right there."

"Have fun," I said.

She nodded, then left my office. At the door, she paused and said, "Bob's already gone, so it's just you. Don't forget the alarm."

"I'm leaving in ten or fifteen minutes," I said, "And I've been setting that alarm since you were in diapers."

After she was gone, it was remarkable how a place that was normally so active could be so quiet. I was rarely there after our regular business hours, and the entire building had an eerie silence to it that caught me by surprise. It was no place for me to be alone tonight. I locked up my office, then hesitated in the hallway upstairs by the window that looked down on the back parking lot.

Dusk was nearing, but Andrew Joy was out there with a shovel, attacking the last bit of free ground on his property. What an odd bird.

I locked the place up, happy to be free of it for the night. Once I was back in my apartment, snug with a hamburger and *Twelve Angry Men* in the VCR, my life felt more normal than it had all day. For the rest of the evening I tried to forget about Kelly, about Earnest Joy, and about the unwanted fence, and thanks to Henry Fonda and company, I almost managed to do it.

SIX

∘ ∘ ∘

I was shaving the next morning when the phone rang. Who in the world could be calling me so early?

"Hello," I said, getting some shaving cream on the receiver by accident.

"Ben, this is Bob. You need to get down here right now."

I couldn't remember my calm and tranquil brother ever sounding so agitated in my life. "Where are you, and what's going on?"

"I'm at the shop. Andrew Joy's been busy. Part of our back parking lot's been destroyed."

"I'll be right there," I said. I hurriedly finished shaving and got dressed. Had Earnest's murder driven Andrew over the edge?

He knew perfectly well we were disputing his family's claim on our land. Why would he escalate what was already an acrimonious situation? By the time I got to the soap shop, I was ready for a fight. If I had to stand in front of him with a shovel of my own to stop him, I'd do it.

I parked in the side lot and hurried toward the back. There were a couple of industrial-sized trucks parked on Joy land, and it only took a second to realize they were from the same company that had installed the fence. I wondered what he was doing now. Had Andrew decided to electrify the installation after all?

Instead, to my great surprise, they were actually starting to take it down.

"What's going on?" I asked the two-man crew as they worked.

"We got orders to remove it," one of the workers said. "It was some kind of emergency, from what we were told."

"Who did you speak to?" I asked.

One of the men looked at the other and asked, "Did you catch her name, Billy? She was pretty strong with her demands. Even offered to pay us double-time if we did it this morning. We weren't about to pass that up, were we, Billy?" He lowered his voice as he added, "Listen, buddy, I'm sorry if you're unhappy about this thing coming down, but we do what we're told."

"Her last name didn't happen to be Perkins, did it?" Had one of my sisters—or worse yet, my mother—ordered the fence's removal? What if the Joy claim was legitimate? Did that make us criminally liable in some way? I wished I could call Kelly, and I would if things got any worse.

The fence man shook his head. "Like I said, I didn't catch her name. You might want to move out of the way," he told me. "We're about ready to take it down."

As they started removing the fencing, I looked around for my brother. Bob's truck was in the lot beside my Miata, but he was nowhere to be seen. I was about to go inside Where There's Soap to look for him when I saw the back door open. Bob walked down the steps, and to my surprise, Terri was right on his heels.

I walked toward them, past where one of the buried posts used to be. "What's going on here?"

Bob said, "Terri's dropping the whole thing after what Andrew did last night."

"What did he do?" I asked as my gaze caught sight of one area of our parking lot. A spot had been dug up in the old asphalt and the dirt from the hole was spread around it. A compact car would have fit inside it—though it was only six inches deep—and I saw tread tracks in the dirt. He'd actually used a bulldozer, and from the look of things, it appeared that Andrew had planned to expand his garden on our land.

"Has he lost his mind?" I asked as I walked over to the hole. "Sorry," I added when I looked back at Terri.

"Believe me, I've been asking myself the same thing. I was out jogging this morning and I found him digging in the dirt with a piece of heavy equipment. We had it out, and I told him enough was enough."

"And he agreed with you?" I asked. I couldn't imagine Andrew backing down after the squabble we'd had.

"He didn't have any choice," Terri said. "We just found out that I'm the executor of Dad's estate, to my brother's great distress. I told him if he didn't drop this right here and now, he wouldn't see a dime of Joy money until he was too old to enjoy it." She had something in her hand and gave it to me. "This is for you."

I took the faded piece of paper from her and saw my grandfather's shaky signature on the hand-printed IOU. "Are you sure about this?" I asked.

"I'm positive," she said. "I want the chance to make this

right again between us. It doesn't matter what happened in the past. All that counts now is how we go on from here."

The fence installers—actually, the uninstallers would be more appropriate—removed the last post, and all that was left to show what had happened was a series of holes in our lot. Granted one was big enough to park the Miata in, but it was our land again, undisputed.

"Why did he start digging there?" I asked, curious about his choice. The spot where he'd dug was a good seven feet from the edge of the asphalt, and it looked like a random place to start to me.

"Who knows what he was thinking," Terri said. "I'd make him come over and apologize in person, but I'm afraid that's where he'd draw the line. My apology will have to be enough."

I offered her my hand. "That's good enough for me. As for me, I'm sorry about the way I've been acting, too."

A pair of big trucks came rumbling up the road, and I was surprised when they pulled into the back lot. They were from Hitch Paving and Asphalt, and as soon as they stopped, six men hopped out of the cabs.

Terri said, "I almost forgot. I'm having the back lot paved at my expense for all your trouble. I hope that's all right."

Bob smiled. "Are you kidding? That's great. Isn't it, Ben?"

"It's awfully generous," I said. "You didn't have to do that. Having them work on Sunday must be costing you a fortune."

"It's not costing me a dime," she said, smiling. "It's taken care of."

Bob slapped my shoulder. "Don't ask questions, Ben, just say thank you."

"Thank you," I said.

"You're most welcome. Now if you two will excuse me, I'm not finished with my brother just yet." She gestured to his rambling garden and added, "I'm getting tired of dodging gopher holes, so I've called a landscaper to come in and plow this mess under and turn it back into a lawn."

I grinned. "Can I be with you when you tell Andrew about it?" The man's head would absolutely explode when he found out his horticultural days were over.

"I don't think so," she said. Terri started back toward the jewelry shop when she hesitated and turned back to me. "Are we okay now, Ben?"

"This should take care of it," I said. "Thanks again."

"It never should have gotten this far," she said.

After she was gone, Bob smacked my arm. "Can you believe this? You're going to look like a hero to everybody in our family."

"What are you talking about?" I asked as I watched the men fill in the holes prior to paving the lot.

"Terri told me inside that the only reason she did this was because of you. Do you mind explaining what you said to her?"

"I can't imagine," I said. "I honestly don't have a clue what she's talking about."

He slapped my arm again. "Now's not the time to be modest, Ben. You need to call Mom and tell her right now. She'll be thrilled."

"You can call her if you'd like," I said. "I want to watch this."

"Okay," he said, "But I'm giving you all the credit."

After Bob went back into the shop, I watched as the crew began to pave the lot. Terri had acted quickly enough once she'd learned she had the power to give orders. I was sure Andrew had put up more of a fight than she'd admitted, but at least we had our lot back. I looked at the IOU in my hand, thought about shredding it, then decided to give Paulus the honor of destroying himself. There was no doubt in my mind that it was authentic; it was his signature, no matter how shaky the lettering was. Was he drunk when he'd signed it? No doubt he had been, given his vague recollection of the event. But that didn't matter now. My grandfather had stopped drinking right after the incident, and if it had saved his life, it had been worth it even if the Joys had taken the whole building.

By the time I left the shop that evening, shining black asphalt covered the back parking lot, and the customer lot, too. I'd tried to protest that it was too much, but the foreman had informed me that he had the materials on his truck, and it would be too big a headache to find a place to dump them. All we needed was a fresh set of lines, and we'd be set with both our parking lots. The parking lots were in stark contrast with what they'd been that morning. Terri had made more than a good faith effort, and I was going to make sure every Perkins knew about it, and accepted the gesture for what it was: a chance to make things right between us again.

AS a nice change of pace, the next day I managed to prepare the classroom well before my students showed up for their second session learning how to hand-mill their own soaps. Though it was great having the back parking area again, there was still something a lot more serious hanging over my head at the moment than where to stow the Miata. Molly honestly considered me one of her chief suspects in

Earnest Joy's murder, and I was going to have to do something about that, and soon.

I was just coming out of the classroom when I bumped into Diana from the bookstore again. "Good morning," I said. "Did you do something different with your hair?"

"I'm trying out a new style," she said as she tilted her head to the side. "What do you think?"

I nodded. "Well, if my vote counts, I like it."

I saw dimples I'd missed before as she smiled. "It counts a lot. Thanks. Ben, I'm really looking forward to today's class."

"It appears that the soapmaking bug has bitten you."

She smiled. "I've always loved crafting, and it's a real added bonus when I can use what I make. I can't wait to see how my efforts on Friday turned out."

I looked around, but no one else was there yet. "Why don't we check now?"

"Really? That would be great."

I led her back into the classroom, then shut the door so none of my other students saw that I was already there. I had no interest in holding court before the session, as I'd done a few times in the past.

I found Diana's name on a mold, then tried to slide her soap out of the cylinder. It wouldn't budge.

"Did I do something wrong?" she asked, concern thick in her voice.

"Not necessarily. Sometimes the soap's a little finicky about coming out. Let's try something." I popped the mold in a mini freezer tucked under one of the cabinets and said, "Let's give it a few minutes and then we'll try again."

"I figured you'd run hot water over it," she said.

"We don't want to dilute your pretty soap. So how's the book business?"

She smiled. "It's good, but sometimes it's nice to get away. I imagine you feel the same way working here all the time, don't you?"

"Absolutely," I agreed. "Sometimes I wonder if we own the business or the business owns us."

"Exactly. It's nice to have a conversation about running a business with someone who knows what I'm talking about."

I glanced at the clock on the wall and said, "Let's check that mold."

I retrieved it from the freezer, and this time the soap slid right out onto my hand.

She took the oatmeal-toned soap log and admired it for a second. "That's really neat. Can I use it right away?"

"We'll go over this in class, but you need to cut it into disks, then cure it on a drying rack. Three weeks is ideal, but you can bump it up a little if you're in a rush."

"Wow, I didn't have any idea it took that long," she said as the classroom door opened and Cindy walked in.

My youngest sister said, "Ben, there's . . . oops, sorry, I should have knocked."

Before she could close the door again, I said, "Cindy, this is Diana. I'm sure you saw her in class on Friday. She's one of our students, and she owns that cool bookstore I was telling you about the other day."

Cindy smiled at her, then said, "It's nice to meet you. Sorry, I didn't mean to interrupt."

"You weren't," I protested. "What's going on?"

"There's a phone call for you, Ben."

I turned to Diana. "I'd better take this."

"Go right ahead. Do you mind if I stay in here until class gets started?"

"Be my guest," I said. "I shouldn't be long."

When Cindy and I were out in the boutique, I said, "Don't say a word. I was just letting her see her soap."

"Benjamin Perkins, I wasn't going to say a thing." I didn't believe her for a second, so I wasn't surprised when she added, "Is she doing something different with her hair? I could swear I smelled perfume, too. Obsession, I think it's called."

I shook my head. "If she's wearing something, I missed it. As for her hair, she wanted to try something new. Now who's on the phone?"

Cindy smiled. "I don't have a clue. They asked for you, and I'm not the nosy type."

"Of course not," I said, shaking my head. I picked up the phone and introduced myself.

A woman's voice said, "Mr. Perkins, this is Trudy Lowery, and I've got some delightful news for you. I'm happy to inform you that you've won a prize at the raffle held at the Fair on the Square this past weekend."

"Great, I bet it's something I really need. It's a pedicure, isn't it?"

She hesitated, obviously expecting a little more excitement than I'd been able to muster. After a slight pause, she said, "No, I'm sorry, that's not what you won at all. If that's what you were hoping for, perhaps you could trade prizes with the woman who won the beauty treatment."

"No thanks. I'm actually kind of happy I won the stuffed armadillo instead." I don't know why I'd said it even as I did, but for some odd reason, my earlier conversation with Diana had lightened my mood enough to be playful with this stranger.

I could hear her riffling through some pages when she finally said, "Mr. Perkins, we didn't raffle an armadillo this year. In fact, to my knowledge, we never have."

"Then I don't have much chance of winning it, do I?"

That seemed to confuse her even more. "This *is* Benjamin Perkins, isn't it?"

"Yes, ma'am, it is."

After another hesitation, she asked, "And you did enter a raffle on Saturday?"

This had gone on long enough. "I entered one ticket in each of the pickle jars, but to be honest with you, I didn't even look at the prizes you were giving away. I'm sorry for the confusion. So what did I win?"

With new energy in her voice, she said, "You've been chosen to receive a complimentary dinner for two at The Lakefront Inn."

Wonderful. The food was excellent there, and the ambiance was the best there was in Harper's Landing. Unfortunately, it was also the place Kelly and I had gone on our first date.

"That's fine," I said, not able to hide my disappointment.

The woman said, "Honestly, it's quite nice. My husband took me there on our anniversary."

"Fine. Okay, thanks for calling."

I was about to hang up when she said, "Mr. Perkins? I'm afraid there's a stipulation to your prize."

"What's that?" I asked.

She hemmed and hawed, then finally admitted, "The dinner's for tonight. I'm sorry about the short notice, but it is a stipulation for the prize."

"Of course it is," I said a little louder than I should have. Kelly wasn't an option for a dinner date anymore, and neither was Molly. I wasn't about to take one of my sisters or my mother. Maybe I'd give the whole thing to Bob. His wife deserved a nice meal out, and they could celebrate their wonderful news in style. "Do I need a coupon or anything?"

"No, just show your driver's license to the maitre d' and you're set."

"Do you mean I can't give it to someone else?" I asked.

She hesitated, then said, "I'm sorry, but it's nontransferable. You'll have a delightful time, I'm sure of it."

"Dinner for one at a fancy restaurant? What's not to like?"

She laughed. "Didn't I say? It's a meal for two, so feel free to bring a date."

"If I can scare one up, I will." I hung up, wondering what I was going to do. There was no way I was passing up a free meal at The Lakefront. Though Kelly had insisted on paying during our date, I'd left the tip and it had still put a dent in my weekly budget. It looked like I was going to be taking Mom after all when Diana walked up. "Ben, I have a question for you."

Should I ask her to join me? Why not? "Okay, but I want to ask you something first. How would you like to have dinner with me tonight at The Lakefront Inn?"

"I'd love to," she said before I could barely get the words out of my mouth.

I quickly added, "I just won a free dinner from the raffle Saturday, and I have to use it tonight or lose it."

Diana frowned. "I must admit, I've had more romantic propositions in my life. You are asking me out on a date, aren't you?"

Was I? Kelly had broken up with me, and Molly would probably never be any more than a great friend. So why shouldn't I start dating again? I'd felt a spark with Diana from the first time we'd met.

I must have taken too long to answer. She said softly, "Ben, if you've changed your mind about asking me, that's fine. Just don't leave me up in the air like this, okay?"

I smiled at her and took her hands in mine. "I'm sorry. I'm just a little out of sorts today. Can I try it again?"

That brought her smile back. "Absolutely." She made no move to pull her hands away from mine.

"Diana, would you like to go out with me tonight on a date to The Lakefront Inn?"

She pretended to think about it, started to shake her head, then began to laugh. "That's much better. Yes, I'd love to go out with you tonight."

Her enthusiasm wiped away my last doubt. "Then it's a date. You won't have any problem getting away from the bookstore, will you?"

Diana smiled. "For dinner with you at The Lakefront, I'd close my doors if I had to. I can't wait."

"It sounds like fun," I agreed.

Some of the members of my class were milling about the shop, and I saw that it was five minutes until we needed to get started. I caught Cindy's smile and realized she'd witnessed my entire bungling attempt to ask Diana out. I figured I might as well take the abuse from her up front, so I said, "Would you excuse me for a minute?"

Diana nodded happily, and I walked over to my sister. "Go ahead, get it out of your system."

Cindy tried to look innocent, but it was beyond her range as an actress. "Whatever do you mean?"

"You heard me foul that up. Blast away."

Cindy shook her head. "I'd be the first to admit that you used a technique I've never seen before, but she said yes, so I figure that's a success, don't you?"

"That's it? That's the best you can do?" I knew my family too well to think I was going to get off that easily.

Cindy said, "Ben, I think it's wonderful. From what I've heard about Diana around town, I think she's actually a better fit for you than Kelly ever was."

I didn't even know where to start in replying to that, so I just shook my head and walked away. Before I could get to the classroom door, I heard Cindy talking to Kate and Louisa. "You all are not going to believe what our big brother just did."

They were both listening raptly when I announced that class would begin in one minute. That broke up their chat as effectively as a bucket of cold water, since Cindy was assisting me.

I was walking to the front of the classroom when Cindy called out, "Hang on a second, Ben. You've got another phone call."

"Take a message and I'll call them back," I said. "I'm just getting ready to get started."

"It's Grandpa," she said. "From the sound of his voice, you need to talk to him."

I walked back to the counter and said, "Fine, I'll talk to him, but that means you have to start teaching the class by yourself until I'm through."

"No way," she said. "That wasn't part of our deal."

"Sorry, but you have to do it." I looked around and saw that Louisa and Kate were both waiting on customers. "It shouldn't be that bad. I shouldn't be long."

She reluctantly agreed, then said, "What should I do?"

"Help them get their soaps out of the molds, teach them how to cut and cure them. I should be back before you're finished."

"And what if you're not?" she asked. There was a real look of terror on her face.

"Listen to me, Cindy. You are a wonderful soapmaker, and you have it in you to be an excellent teacher. Trust your instincts. Show them some of the blends you've made in the past. They want to learn, and they're eager for you to teach them."

She hesitated. "But I could never do what you do."

"And you shouldn't. Find your own style. Remember, I believe in you. Now from what you said, I've got to take this call. Go on in there. Your class is waiting for you."

I walked behind the desk, but I didn't pick the telephone up until I watched Cindy walk inside. It was a trial by fire, and not one that I had arranged for her, but I knew if she could get through the first two minutes, she'd be fine. Paulus was just going to have to wait. I counted to 120, then I walked over and cracked open the door.

Cindy was showing Herbert Wilson how to free his soap, and Constance was adding her own direction. My littlest sister turned to her and said, "Constance, it looks like Myra's having a little trouble in back. Could you be a sweetheart and help her?"

Constance nodded vigorously. "I'd be delighted." After she was gone, I saw Herbert wink at Cindy and I knew my sister had crossed that particular hurdle.

By the time I got back to the phone, the line was dead. I was sure that whatever Paulus had wanted hadn't been all that urgent. If it was, he'd surely have held on the line. Then again, if he'd had to go in a hurry, I knew my grandfather would call back. I was tempted to sneak inside and watch Cindy teach, but I knew she needed the chance to try it solo first, just to prove to herself that she could do it.

The phone rang again, and I picked it up. "Where There's Soap," I said, as was our custom at the shop.

"Good, I found you," my grandfather said. "Where were you?"

"I was just getting ready to teach a class. Sorry about that. What's going on?"

There was a level of enthusiasm in my grandfather's voice I hadn't heard in years. "Ben, I think I'm on to something."

"What are you talking about?"

"What do you think, boy? I'm talking about Earnest's murder. I've been digging into it, and I'm learning some pretty fascinating stuff about the man."

My grandfather was not the subtlest of men. It worried me that he wasn't taking the proper precautions when it came to nosing into other people's lives. "I didn't realize you were looking into it."

He laughed. "You're not the only Perkins who's good at snooping. I'm surprised how much fun it is."

"You're being careful, aren't you?" I asked. "This isn't a game, you know."

"Ben, I was able to stay out of trouble for well over forty years before you were even born. I know how to watch my step."

I wasn't sure I believed him. "Why don't we work on it together? We can share our thoughts, and that way we can look out for each other at the same time."

He snorted into the phone. "I don't need a babysitter, either. I just wanted you to know what I was doing."

I had to be careful; I could tell he was feeling defensive. "I'm talking about teamwork, Paulus, just like we have running the shop. We need to work together on this. So what have you found out?"

"Well, I've uncovered some pretty fascinating stuff. Have you had a real look at some of the jewelry in the Joy store's cases? I was in there this morning—Ben, I've got to go. I'll call you back later."

"Wait, what is it?" I asked, but the line was already dead. Great. As if Molly didn't have enough problems with me digging into her official police inquiries, now she was going to have to contend with Paulus snooping around as well. I loved the enthusiasm I'd heard in my grandfather's voice, but I was worried, too. Even though he was quite a bit older than I was and more experienced in life, he was a neophyte at this, and there weren't many mistakes allowed investigating murders freelance. His snooping added just one more reason why I'd have to get serious about my own investigation if it would help me keep him out of danger. I was concerned enough to consider calling Molly and telling her about Paulus's behavior, but then quickly rejected the idea. The way she'd been acting lately, she'd probably find a reason to lock us both up.

To my surprise, Molly herself walked into the shop twenty seconds after I'd rejected the idea of talking to her.

As she approached me, I could see that she was as displeased about seeing me as I was in finding her at my family's soap shop.

I saw her stop and talk to Louisa a second, who quickly hurried into the back room. After a few seconds, Molly approached me.

"So, are you here to arrest me?" I asked. I was only half joking when I'd said it.

"Why, are you confessing to something?" There wasn't much humor in her voice, either.

"Hardly. I just seem to be the only suspect you're focusing on."

I realized I'd goaded her a little too much as soon as I'd

said it. "Ben, believe it or not, I'm looking at other people close to Earnest Joy. Besides that, I've got other cases I'm working on."

"More important than a homicide? I thought you handled one case at a time." I didn't need Molly distracted. She had to be focused on finding Joy's real killer.

She frowned. "Normally I do, but we seem to be having a crime spree in Harper's Landing at the moment. I'm helping out on an arson investigation and I'm coordinating a counterfeiting task force, too."

"Counterfeiting, here? You're kidding, right? We're not exactly a hotbed of criminal activity, are we?"

She was about to reply when Jeff came out of the back. He smiled the second he saw Molly, then scowled at me. "Would you keep your voice down, Ben? I could hear you all the way in the back."

"She started it," I said.

"I did not," Molly protested.

I hadn't seen Mom lurking in the wings, but she had to have been nearby, she got there so quickly.

"Molly, I need to see you and Benjamin outside."

Jeff protested, "Mom, we've got a date."

"It can wait. You stay here." She pointed to Molly and me, then said, "Now."

Even though Molly was a seasoned cop and I was a grown man, we both followed her with worried expressions on our faces. My mother was an expert at chewing people out, and it looked like we were both going to get a lecture neither of us wanted.

The day was pleasant out on the porch, but the rocking chairs were empty. At least nobody would witness the castigation. Before she could get started, I said, "I want to say something first."

"I want to go first," Molly said.

"Sit," Mom commanded, and we both did, our protests dying in our throats.

"Molly, I'm disappointed in you." Her words were spoken softly, but there was an edge to them. "You are a professional police officer, and yet I hear you practically shouting at my son from all the way upstairs."

I thought Molly would protest, but she just said, "I'm sorry, ma'am."

I stared over at her, not believing what I'd just heard. She'd never given up in a fight so fast in her life. It was an apology based on appeasement, not sincerity.

I couldn't believe Mom was buying it, but evidently she was. Great. Now it was my turn.

She stared long and hard at me before saying, "You, young man, should know better, too." My mother loomed over me, and there was a real snap to her words. "Are you ever going to grow up?"

"I think I am," I mumbled under my breath.

"What was that?" she asked.

"I said I am."

Mom shook her head. "I sincerely doubt it. I understand you two are going through a rough patch in your relationship, but you need to stop this right now before you kill your friendship completely."

Molly said, "All due respect to you, Mrs. Perkins, but I'm dating Jeff. I don't have a relationship with him." As she said the last word, she pointed in my direction while avoiding eye contact with me.

My mother said, "Molly, a friendship is a relationship, too. You've been in each other's back pockets since kindergarten. I still can't figure out what there is between you, whether it's just friendship as you both so vigorously proclaim or something more, but I do know how important you are to each other. You've got to stop this bickering."

"Then tell her to stop trying to pin a murder on me," I said.

Mom jumped all over that. "Benjamin, you know Molly is fair. She's just doing her job, and you're not making it any easier for her."

"So what do you want me to do, confess to a murder I didn't commit? That would make life easier for everybody but me."

"Don't be flip with me, young man. I expect you to give her the respect she deserves."

Molly had a smug look on her face as I capitulated. "Yes, ma'am."

"And as for you," Mom said as she turned back to Molly, "I hope you find what you're looking for, I sincerely do, but don't trifle with my sons' hearts. Any of them. Do we understand each other?"

Molly paused, then said, "Yes, ma'am, I believe we do."

Mom smiled at us both, then said, "Good, I'm glad we got that settled. Now I understand you have a luncheon date," she said to Molly, who gratefully got up and went back into the shop.

I started to get up, too, when Mom said, "Ben, I'm worried about you."

"What else is new?" I asked, trying to smile as I said it. "That's what you're best at."

As I stood, she hugged me. "No, this is what I'm best at. You've had your world turned upside down in the last few days, haven't you?"

"I've had better weekends," I admitted. "But I'll be all right."

She pulled away and patted my cheek. "I know you will; you're strong. Do you know what you should do?"

"What's that?" I asked, fearful of what was coming.

"You should go out tonight and have a nice time. Try to forget about your troubles. Find someone interesting and ask her out to dinner. You don't have to propose. Just have fun. You deserve it."

I didn't want to admit it, but I knew Mom would find out soon enough. "Actually, I just made a date with one of my soapmaking students. We're going out tonight to The Lakefront Inn."

She had a shocked look on her face, and a part of me wanted to stop my explanation so she could wonder about it for the rest of the day. I couldn't do that to her, though.

After a pregnant pause, I confessed, "I won a free dinner for tonight from the raffle Saturday, so I'm taking Diana Long out. She owns Dying To Read in town."

"The mystery bookstore? I've been meaning to go in there. I hear it's fabulous."

"You should, it's really something. So are we finished here?"

Mom nodded. "I'm sorry about how I acted earlier. I hated to treat you two like children, but somebody had to say something."

"You did the right thing," I said, "But if you tell Molly I said that, I'll deny it with my last breath."

She pinched my cheek, something she knew I hated but did occasionally nonetheless. "Don't ever change, Benjamin."

"I thought you just ordered me to." I skipped away from her half-hearted swipe, and even managed to get her to laugh. It died in her throat as we saw Jeff and Molly drive away. They'd gone out the back door, no doubt to avoid running into me.

Mom shook her head. "I do hope they know what they are doing."

"We're all grown-ups," I said, "regardless of how we've been acting lately."

"I wish I could be sure of that," she said as we both walked inside. Two sisters and two brothers were standing near the register when we walked back in, no doubt trying to catch a glimpse of the inquisition that had been going on outside.

Mom clapped her hands together. "The break's over. Everyone, let's get to work."

Bob and Jim disappeared into the back while Louisa and Kate busied themselves straightening the shelves. Mom smiled. "That's what I like, a family that listens. Now I've got to get back upstairs. I've got a pile of paperwork on my desk."

As she started for the back stairs, I called out, "Hey Mom."

"Yes," she said as she turned.

"Thanks."

"You're most welcome. Have a lovely time tonight, Benjamin."

"I'm planning to," I said.

The second Mom was through the door, Kate and Louisa nearly tackled me.

Kate said, "Come on, big brother, give. What happened out there?"

"What are you talking about?" I asked as innocently as I could manage.

"You know exactly what I want to know," she said.

I looked over at Louisa. "You, too?"

She just smiled. "Mom's scoldings are great, as long as you're not the one on the receiving end. Was it bad?"

I studied their eager faces, then said, "I don't know what you two are talking about. We had a pleasant conversation, then Molly left to have lunch with Jeff."

Kate stuck her tongue out at me. "Spoilsport."

Louisa just laughed as she locked her arm in her sister's. "Come on, we're not going to get anything out of him. Let's inventory our shelf stock while it's quiet, and maybe both of us will get out of here before nine tonight."

"But I want to talk to Ben about his big date tonight," Kate protested.

Louisa answered, "Do you honestly think he's going to tell us anything more about that than he did about what happened on the porch? Come on, Sis, get serious."

"All right," she agreed reluctantly.

I mouthed a silent thank you to Louisa, who just winked back at me. I knew I'd have to go through a grilling session tomorrow about dinner tonight, but at least I'd been spared a cross-examination before I'd even actually done anything.

SEVEN

• • •

I glanced at my watch and saw that it was past time for class to dismiss. Was Cindy keeping an eye on the clock? I waited four more minutes, then started for the classroom door just as it opened.

Diana was the first one out. "What happened to you, stranger?"

"I got hung up," I said. "Sorry about that. How was the class?"

"Your sister seemed nervous at first, but she did fine once she got into it. She's really very good. Will you be there tomorrow?"

"I'll do my best not to miss it," I said. "Listen, what time would you like me to pick you up? Would a late dinner work better for you or an early one? I'm pretty flexible."

She smiled at me and said, "I don't get a lot of chances to go out at night because of the bookstore, especially to a place as nice as The Lakefront. Let's make it seven, shall we?" She handed me a slip of paper with her address and telephone number on it. "If I don't hear from you, I'll expect to see you at seven." She added, "Thanks again for the invitation. I can't wait."

"It sounds great to me, too."

As Diana was leaving, I noticed Kate and Louisa were watching us. I just shook my head and walked into the classroom, doing my best to pretend that they weren't there.

Herbert and Constance Wilson had been talking to Cindy, but they broke away and we met halfway to the door.

"Did you enjoy class today?" I asked them.

Herbert winked at me as he said, "Are you kidding? She's better than you are."

Constance smacked his arm. "I can't believe you just said that. Apologize this instant."

He nodded, then said, "Ben, I'm sorry I told you the truth. It won't happen again." There was another wink for my benefit.

"Herbert Wilson, you know that's not what I meant."

"Woman, give me some peace."

They were still squabbling as they left. Cindy was at one of the stations cleaning up. I was getting the royal frost treatment from her, but I wasn't about to let her stay mad at me.

"So how'd it go?" I asked.

"It was fine," she said curtly without looking up.

"Come on, I heard you were fantastic! Well done, Sis. I'm proud of you."

She looked up at me and said, "Benjamin Perkins, you set me up. I can't believe my own grandfather had a hand in it. That phone call was pretty conveniently timed, don't you think?"

"Cindy, I know it might have looked that way, but I swear to you, today's absence was unplanned. He needed to talk to me, and by the time we were through, you were handling things so well I didn't want to interrupt."

Some of the frost was melting, but there was still a chill in her voice. "It could have been a disaster, you know that, don't you?"

I smiled at her. "Not on your life. I've got faith in you, Cindy. I knew you could do it."

"Well, they seemed to like it," she reluctantly admitted.

"The important question here is how you felt about it."

She thought about it for a few moments, then said, "I loved it. I didn't want to, and the last thing in the world I want to do is admit it to you, but I had a blast."

"That's great," I said. "Do you want to teach tomorrow solo, or should I sit in and help you?"

"Let me think about it," she said. "It really was fun."

"Don't sound so surprised. Why do you think I've been teaching all these years?"

Mom walked in and asked, "What's this I hear about you teaching a class today, Cindy ?"

"It's not that big a deal," she said nonchalantly. "Ben needed me to take over, so I handled things here."

Mom hugged her, and I could hear the breath swoosh out of Cindy's lungs. "I knew you could do it. I'm so proud of you."

Cindy pulled back and smiled as she asked, "Proud enough to give me the rest of the day off?"

I knew she must have lost her mind. Mom didn't give away free time unless it was absolutely required. To my shock, Mom clapped her hands together and said, "Why not? Enjoy yourself. You earned it."

"Thanks," Cindy said as she grabbed her coat and ran for the door, no doubt hoping to get there before Mom came to her senses.

"What was that all about?" I asked.

"She had a great triumph today, Benjamin; she deserves a reward."

"What about me? Do I get to leave early, too? After all, I'm the one who talked her into teaching."

She patted my shoulder on her way out the classroom door. "And a fine job you did at that. Unfortunately, with Cindy gone, I need you to help cover the sales floor. Well done, Benjamin."

I laughed as I walked into the boutique section of our operation. My mother had found a way to get exactly what she wanted, seemingly without effort. I was being set up—no doubt by my sisters wanting a captive to grill about his life—but there was absolutely nothing I could do about it but smile.

"Good news, ladies," I said to my two remaining sisters. "It appears that this is your lucky day. I'm working with you two this afternoon."

Kate looked at Louisa and asked, "It's too late to call in sick, isn't it?"

Louisa laughed. "I feel something coming on myself." Two fake coughs were followed by, "I'm not well, not well at all."

"Both of you are ungrateful shrews," I said with a smile. "But I'll ignore your pettiness and help anyway."

They both collapsed against me laughing, until Mom walked out of the break room. "What is this? No foolishness during business hours," she commanded, though her eyes were twinkling. I knew she loved having us all working at Where There's Soap together, and while we'd never get rich doing it, we were just as glad to be there.

After Mom disappeared in back, my sisters fell on me like a shroud. "Come on, Ben. We want details," Kate said.

"I'm not sure what you're talking about," I answered as innocently as I could muster.

Louisa smiled. "I'm sure if you use your imagination, you'll be able to come up with the topic. So what made you ask Diana out? Not that we don't approve, mind you, it's just a little out of character for you to act with such swiftness in your love life."

I stared at them a few seconds, but it was obvious I wasn't going to get any peace until I gave them both something. I took a deep breath, then said, "I won a dinner at the raffle, and I had to take it tonight. Diana was here, so I asked her. Satisfied?"

Kate looked at Louisa and said, "Do you buy that for one second?"

"It's lame enough to be true," she said. "Or did he make up the raffle win as an excuse to ask her out?"

"Good point," Kate said as she turned to me. "Well, did you?"

"Ladies, do you honestly think I'd choose The Lakefront if I was going to fake a free dinner?"

Louisa laughed. "True, The Hound Dog would have been a better choice. Well, cheaper, anyway."

"Are you two finished now? I for one would like to get some work done."

They finally agreed to relent, and I set about working in the boutique. For the rest of the afternoon, I helped customers with their selections of molds, base soap, aromatics, and emollients. Lately I didn't often get to work the floor, and it was a real pleasure spending time there.

A woman in her late fifties came in late in the day sporting teased hair and spandex. She didn't look like the typical soapmaker, but then again, we saw a range of customers at Where There's Soap, and I'd learned early on not to judge people by their appearances.

I noticed as she asked Kate a question, and my sister pointed straight at me. As the woman approached, I could see Kate's grin. It was all I could do to keep from sticking my tongue out at my sister.

As the woman neared me with her right hand extended, she said, "My name's Linda Mae, and I want to shake your hand."

"Okay," I said warily, doing as she asked. "May I ask why?"

She smiled broadly. "You surely can, Darlin'. I hear you're the one who finally took care of Ernie."

I pulled my hand back. "You heard wrong."

She looked surprised by my reaction. "You mean you didn't do it?"

"No, ma'am, I did not. Sorry to disappoint you."

She shrugged. "Life's full of disappointment, isn't it? At least somebody did it, and whoever it was, I hope and pray I have the chance to shake his hand someday."

It was a pretty callous attitude. "How well did you know Earnest Joy?" I asked.

She snorted. "Long enough to be married to him for eleven months. That man was meaner than a snake. You did the world a favor."

"I keep telling you; I didn't do anything," I insisted. "When were you divorced?"

She winked at me. "Now who ever said we were divorced?"

That was a shocker. "Funny, I didn't hear your name being mentioned in the will," I said.

She frowned, crinkling her nose at the same time.

"Yeah, that's why I came to town. Ernie and I kept separate households, so to speak, but I've got the wedding papers, and they're as legal as can be. I'm going to get my share, you can believe that."

"I don't have anything to do with any of that," I said, trying to back up a few steps in case her taste in clothes or basic insanity was contagious.

"Don't fret about it," she said. "I've got a lawyer of my own. Well, if you're not the man deserving of my thanks, I'll just head on out."

Kate waited until Linda Mae was gone, then came up to me and said, "What was that all about?"

"Let me ask you something. Did you know Earnest Joy was married?"

She said, "Sure. Terri and Andrew's mom died ages ago, though."

"Apparently he married Linda Mae later."

Kate looked puzzled. "So why did she want to see you?"

"I'd tell you, but it sounds too crazy to believe," I said.

"Try me, Ben."

I bit my lip, then admitted, "She said she wanted to shake the hand of the man who killed her husband."

Kate shivered noticeably. "That's dreadful. I almost feel bad for Earnest."

"It's tough, I'll grant you that. Still, there's a part of me that thinks she's exactly what he deserved. It would be nice to believe that she managed to make him just a little miserable while he was alive; he spread so many dark clouds himself."

She put a hand on my arm. "Ben, I can't stop you from thinking it, but you shouldn't say things like that. It could get you into real trouble, given Molly's suspicions. There's no reason to give her more cause to think you might have done it, and bad-mouthing a dead man would surely get her attention."

I scratched my chin. "It's hard to imagine being in much deeper than I am now, but thanks for the advice. I'll try to watch what I say."

She nodded, then walked back to the register, and I started waiting on legitimate customers again.

By closing time, I'd made my share of sales. Kate looked at Louisa and said, "He really wasn't nearly as bad as I thought he'd be. What do you think?"

"He's got potential," she said. "But he's going to need a lot of work."

I shook my head. "Say what you want. I was magnificent, and you both know it."

They were still laughing as I left.

It was time to get ready for my date. I was old enough to know better, but as I showered and dressed, I still couldn't keep the butterflies out of my stomach. I hadn't wanted to abandon my budding relationship with Kelly, but ending it hadn't been my choice. Molly had always offered a safe and comfortable evening when I needed it, but that wasn't an option anymore, either. Ready or not, tonight I was embarking on a new relationship, and I wasn't about to let what had happened in the past—no matter how recently—affect it.

It was time for a fresh start.

I got to Diana's apartment ten minutes early, so I parked out front and tried to sit patiently until it was time to ring her doorbell. I'd run the Miata through the car wash in town on the way over to her place, and it gleamed. Five minutes that seemed like a month later, I finally walked to her door. Before I could even knock, it opened.

She looked absolutely lovely. Her lustrous brown hair was curled and wavy, and she'd done something with her makeup to really make her eyes dance. It didn't hurt that the burgundy dress accentuated her curves perfectly.

Without stopping to censor my reaction, I said, "Wow."

She smiled brightly. "For such a short sentence, that's the nicest thing anybody's said to me in ages."

"You look great," I added lamely.

"Thank you. I love that suit."

I nodded my acceptance of her compliment. "Nothing but the best for The Lakefront, right?"

"Absolutely," she said as we walked out together. "This is going to be so much fun."

"I think so, too."

She looked at my Miata and said, "It's my turn to say Wow. I love your car."

"Thanks. I'm pretty attached to it, too." I held the door open for her, and she graciously accepted the courtesy for what it was.

As we drove to the restaurant, I asked, "So how did you happen to own a bookstore?"

"My parents died when I was nine years old, and I found my solace in books. Charlotte MacLeod, Carolyn Hart, Agatha Christie; they all saved me. I never wanted to do anything else with my life but share my favorite mystery writers with the world. As soon as I turned twenty-one, I got my inheritance, and that's when I opened Dying To Read."

"It must have been tough, losing them like that."

She sighed. "The worst part of it was that I didn't have

any brothers or sisters. Sometimes I feel all alone in the world. I really envy you your family, Ben. It must be heaven."

I'd never heard it described quite like that, but then I'd never met anyone with Diana's unique perspective before, either. "It can be that, but we manage to visit the other place often enough, too."

She laughed. "I've seen the way you all interact. I've always longed for that. So, how do you like working in the family business? I can tell from your class that you truly love to make soap."

"I do," I admitted. "It's a passion of mine. All of us share it, really, though Cindy's not so sure it's what she wants to do with her life yet."

"Really?" she asked. "She's a wonderful teacher. I was quite impressed with her today, once she got warmed up."

"We'll see," I said as I pulled into the parking lot of the restaurant. I felt a little wave of despair as I remembered the last and only other time I'd eaten there. Kelly and I had really enjoyed ourselves, and I wondered if I should have taken Diana somewhere else for our first date, despite the free meal.

She'd been looking out at the rose garden when she caught my eye. "Ben, is everything all right?"

"It's great," I said, trying to put the past behind me and focus on the future.

As we walked in, I admired the heart pine floors, the ceiling, and the delicate flowered wallpaper again. It was as elegant a place as ever. Several of the Shaker-style tables were full. The same short little man with the elegant mustache I'd seen on my last visit was standing at the front, as if he were waiting just for us.

"Welcome back, sir," he said with great enthusiasm.

I was surprised he'd even recognized me. "Hello. I was told to tell you that I'm your raffle winner from the Fair."

He looked delighted by the news. "Excellent, excellent. I'm so happy one of our regular patrons won! Come in, come in, we've got a special table reserved for you. Everything is included in making this evening yours, from cocktails to dessert. There is one stipulation you might not be aware of, though," he said as he looked me sternly in the eye.

So there was a catch after all. "What's that?"

"You are our guests, from the serving staff to my humble self. Please don't insult us by leaving a tip. This evening, you are both members of our family. Agreed?"

"How can I say no to that?" I said.

He smiled broadly. "Excellent. If you'll come with me?"

The elegant little man led us to the best table in the house, positioned by a window with a view of the garden and beyond it, the lake.

As he helped Diana into her chair, he said, "I am Robert. If you need anything, anything at all, I will be offended if you do not ask."

"Thank you, Robert," Diana said in a hushed voice.

After we were alone, she gazed around the room, then said, "I must say, this is the most impressive first date I've ever been on."

"Then I'm glad I bought that ticket. It is nice, isn't it?"

"It's wonderful," she said. "Honestly, I'm usually happy with a diner or cooking at home, but I'm really going to enjoy this."

"So am I," I said. "Thanks for coming on such short notice."

She looked steadily into my eyes, and said, "Thank you for asking. I was hoping we would have the chance to do this sometime."

I smiled. "Well, it's not everyday I get to eat at The Lakefront."

"I'm not talking about that. I would have been just as happy eating at The Hound Dog with you."

"You know what?" I said, enjoying the moment, and very glad I'd asked her. "I feel the same way."

My smile froze in place as I noticed a couple come in the front door. I couldn't believe it for a second, but unfortunately, it was really happening.

Diana asked, "Ben, what's wrong? You look like somebody just walked across your grave."

"It's nothing," I said, trying to recapture my composure.

"Don't tell me that," she said as she casually looked back over her shoulder. After a moment, she said softly, "She's pretty, isn't she?"

At that moment Kelly caught us looking at her, and so did her date. She was out with her ex-husband Wade. Kelly's face fell as she offered us a slight nod. I saw her whisper something to Robert, who glanced our way, then nodded. He led them to the other side of the restaurant, thankfully out of our sight.

Diana asked softly, "So who is she?"

"It's not important. Not anymore."

Diana wasn't about to accept that answer. She put a hand on mine and said, "It's pretty obvious it is. Did you two date?"

I nodded. "Up until pretty recently actually. That's her ex-husband with her. They've decided to reconcile."

"Oh, Ben, I'm sorry."

"No, it's really not important anymore. Let's enjoy our evening, shall we?"

I tried, I honestly did, but our conversation was stilted throughout the salad course and on into the entrée. Diana asked what I thought about Earnest Joy's murder, and that just served to remind me that I was at the top of Molly's list of suspects.

She finished a bite of her salmon, then after a long pause, Diana said, "You know, maybe we should try this another time. I don't blame you, but it's pretty obvious your heart's not into this anymore. Would you like to go?"

"No," I said a little louder than I'd intended. "I want to stay."

Diana raised an eyebrow, then said firmly, "Then you're going to have to do a better job of focusing on me and stop glancing in that direction every twenty seconds. I'm not high maintenance, I promise you that, but I do need some attention when I'm out on a date. Is that fair enough?"

I laughed at her abrupt directness. "I'd say that's more than fair." From that moment on, I started enjoying myself again. The filet mignon was wonderful, and I especially enjoyed the garlic mashed potatoes.

As we waited for our chocolate mousse desserts, a quartet began playing in the other room. "Would you like to dance?"

"I'd love to," she said. As I led her onto the floor, I made sure my gaze never left hers. It was funny, but I'd never danced with a woman as tall as I was before. Most of the time it was easy to forget that Diana was six feet tall, but I found it nice to face her eye-to-eye as we danced. I've never been a fan of skinny women, and she felt full and alive in my embrace as we moved around the dance floor. I swear, it was as if we'd danced together a thousand times before.

After a break in the music, Diana said softly, "I haven't danced nearly enough in my life."

"You really should. You're excellent at it."

As the music started up again, she said, "Not many boys wanted to dance with a girl as tall as they were."

"That was clearly their loss," I said.

After the song ended, I noticed that our desserts had been delivered to our table. "Are you ready for dessert?"

"As long as you promise to dance with me again before we leave."

I nodded. "That's a promise you can be sure I'll keep."

After I led her back to our table, Diana took a bite, and her face lit up. "That is unbelievably good. We'll have to dance till midnight, I've eaten so much."

"I'm game if you are," I said.

To my credit, as we were leaving, I didn't even look around for Kelly and her ex-husband. Not that I didn't think about it, but doing so would have been a disservice to Diana and our evening together.

Robert smiled at us as we approached him. "If you don't mind my saying so, you two are a perfect match. Watching you dance together reminded me of my late wife. I trust everything was to your satisfaction?"

"It was outstanding," I said as I shook his hand. Diana leaned down and kissed his cheek, and to my surprise, Robert's face reddened.

She said, "Thank you for a truly special evening."

"Mademoiselle, you are always welcome here."

As I drove Diana back to her apartment, there was a comfortable silence between us, one that normally took time to develop. I glanced over at her and said, "It was great, wasn't it?"

"I had the time of my life. Honestly, I feel like Cinderella right now."

I looked at my watch. "If that's the case, you're in serious trouble. We're half an hour past your deadline."

"I don't like to think of it as a deadline, more like a suggestion," she said, laughing.

Once we were at her apartment, I walked her to her door, unsure about how to handle the good-night kiss. It had always been the most awkward moment of any first date for me, and that hadn't changed, even though I was a grown man now.

She settled the question for me, turning slowly and offering me a kiss. After a full minute, Diana said, "I hope you had as tenth a good time as I did, Ben."

"I did," I said.

"Then next time I'll treat, but I'm afraid I can't offer you anything as elegant as tonight."

"In all honesty, The Hound Dog is normally more my speed anyway," I said.

"Then we'll try that next. How's Friday sound?"

I shrugged. "I don't know."

She hesitated, then said, "Ben, I'm sorry. I didn't mean to push."

"It's not that," I said. "I'm just not sure I can wait till then to see you again."

Her laughter was infectious. "You'll just have to manage. Besides, I'll see you tomorrow."

"But tomorrow's Tuesday," I said.

"Not for dinner, for class. Surely you haven't forgotten about that."

"To be honest with you, it completely slipped my mind."

This time I kissed her, and it was quite a bit longer than a minute before I let her go.

As I drove back to my apartment, I marveled about how the evening had turned out. There had been a rough patch when Kelly and Wade had walked in, but Diana had stopped me from ruining a wonderful evening. And I'd had a great time, there was no denying it. A slight hint of her perfume lingered in the car, just enough to remind me of our evening together. I was still enjoying the feeling when I walked into my apartment and saw that there was a message on my machine. I hit the play button and heard Kelly's voice.

She managed to choke out, "Ben, I'm so sorry. About everything," before she hung up.

What did she mean by that? Was she sorry she'd nearly ruined my meal, or was she regretting our breakup? Either way, there was nothing I could do about it. I played the message one more time, then hit the erase button.

Still, it managed to steal some of the euphoria I'd been feeling just a few seconds before.

It would be better for me if I could put Kelly behind me and focus on Diana, but I'd never been one to give my heart easily, and it always took me time to rebound. But knowing Diana, she wasn't about to put up with much foolishness on my part.

And that was exactly what I needed at the moment.

THE next morning, thirty minutes before class was due to start, I got a telephone call at Where There's Soap that dramatically altered my plans for the day.

As Cindy and I were preparing for our class—the last one on hand-milling—Kate came into the teaching area.

"Ben, Grandpa is on the phone for you."

Cindy said, "Oh, no, you're not going to do that to me again."

"I'm sure it's nothing," I said as I headed for the door.

"Benjamin, I won't teach this class alone. We'll just cancel and you can help me on the makeup session."

We were going to be teaching our class today to make soaps with ingredients like luffa, peppermint, mango, honey, lavender, and even strawberries. It was the best class to teach, since the students got to decide what kind of soap they wanted to make. We had everything they might want to put in a soap, and our inventory of additives was wide open to them. Half the fun was watching them choose and helping them mold their ideas into reality.

Kate stared at us both, then said, "It's probably nothing. I'm sure it's just a phone call."

Cindy protested, "Yeah, that's what he said yesterday, and I ended up teaching all by myself."

"I couldn't do anything about that," I said, which was not entirely true.

Kate said, "What's the big deal? If Ben can't help you, I'd love to. This is my favorite class session to teach."

"Slow down," I said. "I'm not planning to go anywhere, okay? I'll be right back."

I grabbed the nearest phone and said, "You needed me?"

Paulus had a defeated tone in his voice that shocked me. "Ben, I should have left the detecting to you. I've botched it all up."

"What happened, Paulus?"

He hesitated, then said, "I've been digging into Earnest Joy's murder, and I'm afraid I've attracted the wrong attention. My boy, I could be in some serious trouble."

"Where are you right now?" I asked. I could have Molly there in record time, despite our differences lately. She loved the old man almost as much as I did.

"I'm safe enough, but I'm so paranoid right now, I can't

stop looking over my shoulder. I need you to meet me some-where nearby so we can talk. You have to fix this, Ben."

He'd never asked me for my help in his entire life, and I knew he really was desperate. "Why can't you come here?"

"I don't want anyone to see me going into Where There's Soap, okay? Name someplace else."

I named the first thing I could think of. "Then how about The Hound Dog? Would that do?"

"Yeah, that would be perfect. I'll see you in five minutes."

He hung up before I could say another word. I hurried back to the classroom, and found Kate and Cindy still chatting about hand-milling. "Cindy, I'm sorry, but I've got to bail out on you after all."

"Ben, you can't do this to me."

I met her glare with one of my own. "Our grandfather is in trouble. He needs me."

Kate snapped, "What are you doing standing around here, then? Go. I'll help with the class."

I looked at Cindy and said, "Will you be all right?"

"I'll be fine. She's right. You need to go."

I tore out of there, and jumped into the Miata. It was a short walk to the cafe, but I didn't have the time today. Thankfully there was a parking spot on the street near the diner, and I was there less than two minutes after my phone call with Paulus.

I didn't see his car anywhere nearby, but if he was as paranoid as he'd sounded, my grandfather may have parked pretty far away so no one would know where he was.

Ruby was behind the counter singing along with Elvis. I looked around the diner, but no Paulus.

As "Viva Las Vegas" ended, I asked, "Have you seen Paulus?"

She shook her head. "Not in a few weeks. What's the old scoundrel been up to?"

"I wouldn't mind knowing that myself. I'll just wait on him in a booth."

She cleared a diner's dishes at the counter. "Do you want anything while you're waiting?"

"Why not? Bring me a glass of sweet tea, would you?"

She shot me with a finger. "Coming right your way."

I found a seat where I could watch the front door and look out one of the picture windows at the sidewalk as well. There was light foot traffic outside, and quite a few interesting people passed by, but I only cared about my grandfather. The defeated tone I'd heard in his voice had shaken me more than I wanted to admit. Paulus had always been such a vigorous and vital man. On the phone, he'd sounded beaten, and worse yet, afraid.

Ruby brought me a sweet tea along with a mini pitcher. "I thought you might be thirsty."

"Thanks," I said absently, still staring out the window.

"Ben, is everything okay? You're acting a little odd today."

"I'm fine," I said as I tried to offer her a smile. "Just a little distracted, I guess."

She nodded. "It's a busy world these days, isn't it?" Just then, Elvis started singing about being caught in a trap, and for once, I knew just how he felt.

Ruby's eyes lit up. "I just love this song."

"Is there an Elvis tune you don't?"

She smiled. "No, now that you mention it, I can't say there is."

I waited a good half hour, growing more fidgety by the second. Where was my grandfather? His demand that I meet him had been urgent enough, so why wasn't he there yet? I was getting a bad feeling in the pit of my stomach, and the longer I waited, the worse it got. Where was he? I'd killed my tea and half the pitcher, so the caffeine and sugar were just exacerbating the situation. I should have asked for water, instead.

By the time an hour had passed, I couldn't wait around any longer. It was obvious Paulus, for whatever reason, wasn't going to show up. So where did that leave me? He'd been digging into Earnest Joy's murder, he'd admitted that much to me over the phone yesterday and today. I'd been a little remiss in my own investigation, but it was time to start gearing it up. The reason I hadn't been more adamant about digging deeper into it myself was because there was no way in the world I could believe that Molly might actually think I could have killed the man. I was sure she would do her utmost to prove my innocence, and Molly was the professional, while I was just an amateur dabbling into detection, though I'd had some success in the past.

There was more at stake now, though. Paulus might be in trouble—real or imagined—and if he wasn't going to tell me what he'd done, then I was just going to have to figure it out myself, and try to fix whatever mess he'd claimed he'd made.

The logical place to start digging was at the Joy jewelry store. At least one of Earnest's kids would be there running the place, and it would give me the perfect opportunity to conduct an informal interview. I might even get something out of Andrew or Terri that Molly had missed. Most people were guarded when they talked to the police, but I had a way of listening that encouraged people to open up, and I'd cultivated the talent over the years.

I paid Ruby, then said, "If Paulus shows up, will you tell him to call me on my cell phone?"

"He hates those things and you know it," Ruby said.

"I'm not asking him to use one," I said. "Just have him call me. It's important."

"I'll do it. Are you sure everything's all right?"

I wished I could reassure her with some kind of sincerity, but all I managed was a nod. "I'm just sorry I missed him."

I drove the Miata to the jewelry store, and was glad to see that the parking lot was nearly deserted. That suited me just fine. I didn't want a crowd around while I grilled Earnest's children about his murder, and if they were innocent, I'd do my best to make it up to them. But at the moment, I had a family member at risk myself. That meant that everyone else in the world was fair game.

I was surprised as I walked in to see that there was a sign on the door announcing that the shop closed at one. Those were good hours if you could get them. Then I remembered that their father had just died, and no matter how big a scoundrel I'd thought him to be, his children must have loved him. When I thought about it that way, I was kind of stunned they were even open at all.

I'd been bracing myself for a confrontation with Andrew, but Terri was working by herself at the shop. I knew she'd taken a limited interest in her family's business over the years, preferring to work as a corporate sales rep on the road instead. I wasn't exactly sure what she sold, but I had no doubt she was good at.

"Hi, Ben," Terri greeted me with a smile that seemed sincere enough. "I'm surprised to see you here."

"I'm kind of surprised you're even open."

Terri shrugged as she looked up from an account ledger she'd been studying, a pen poised in her left hand taking copious notes on a legal pad beside it. "I've been trying to decide what to do with this place. Andrew's pressuring me to liquidate all of the assets, but Dad loved this place. I'm thinking about running it myself."

"Could you give up life on the road?" I asked.

"For the right price, I would do it in a heartbeat." She pushed aside the books she'd been peering over and asked, "Is there something I can help you with?"

"I came by to do a little shopping," I said, trying to disguise my real intent.

"So, who's the lucky lady? Is there a new woman in your life, by any chance?"

That caught me off guard. "Now what makes you say that?"

She laughed. "Don't worry, I'm not stalking you or anything like that. You just have that look in your eye."

"What look is that?"

She waved a hand in the air. "New love, at least new interest. So who's the lucky woman?"

She was either the greatest saleswoman in the world, or an extremely talented guesser. The conversation had gotten a little too personal for me, especially since my relationship with Diana was so new that I hadn't been able to define it myself yet. "Let's just leave that a mystery for now, shall we?"

Terri smiled. "That's fine by me. I just love a good mystery. So, let's find something perfect for her, shall we? What are her likes and dislikes?"

"To be honest with you, I'm not really sure." I had come in there to ask questions, and had ended up being grilled instead.

Terri nodded. "Okay, this is going to be a challenge. Let's start with something simple. Does she have pierced ears? Does she like rings, or perhaps necklaces?"

Blast it all, I didn't have a clue. "I don't know. I never really noticed."

"Men," she said. "How do you all manage? Tell you what. Why don't you look around and see if anything strikes your fancy? After that, we can take it from there."

That suited me. I hadn't been all that comfortable under Terri's spotlight, and it felt good to get the focus off my budding love life. I peered into some of the counter displays, and stopped at a bar of gold nestled among pendants and necklaces made with old coins and other golden items. "Is that bar real?"

She laughed. "No, it's spray paint on lead. We couldn't afford a real ingot if we sold the store. It looks nice, though, doesn't it? Dad worked a long time on getting it just right."

There was the opening I'd been hoping for. "Have the police had any luck yet finding out who did it?"

Terri frowned. "Not that I can tell. They've talked to both Andrew and me several times, and I suppose they've interviewed you as well."

Now she was fishing again. "Extensively," I said. "But I didn't do it."

"Neither did we," she answered a little too sharply for my taste, especially since I hadn't accused her of anything. At least not yet.

As casually as I could, I said, "By the way, I met your stepmother the other day."

The distaste on Terri's face was readily apparent. "I heard she was back in town. I never could stand that woman. How did you happen to run into Linda Mae?"

"She came by the soap shop yesterday. It was quite an interesting conversation." That comment drew blood.

Terri's face tightened for just an instant as I said it, but the expression was a microburst of energy, and then she regained her composure.

"Don't believe everything you're told, Ben. That woman would rather lie when the truth would serve her better."

I decided to push a little harder. "I don't know. She made sense to me."

"Then you're both delusional," Terri said curtly.

Instead of replying to that, I decided to change the subject. "Have you seen my grandfather lately?"

She shook her head. "He hasn't been in this shop for years, as far as I know. Why do you ask?"

"No reason," I said. "He just mentioned that he dropped by this week."

"What is this, some kind of game you're playing?" she asked pointedly. "I'm not here the entire time we're open. I'm sure Andrew waited on him, but he didn't come in while I was here." Her eyes narrowed as she asked, "Are you sure you came by looking for a present for your new girlfriend?"

Before I could answer, a voice from the back room said, "Sis, I need to . . ." The rest of his words died in his throat as he spotted me. "What are you doing here?"

"Shopping," I said. It was true, though I was looking for answers instead of jewelry.

"How stupid do you think we are?" he asked.

"I was just talking to your sister about my grandfather. Do you remember what day he came by this week?"

Andrew started to answer when Terri cut him off. "Ben said Paulus told him he was here. When was that, do you remember?"

"We get a lot of customers here," he said. "Perkins, if

you're not going to buy something, why don't you go look somewhere else?"

"That's not very neighborly of you, now is it?"

I could see a vein on Andrew's forehead start to bulge. He wanted me out of there, which was just one more reason I wanted to stay.

"You're free to shop," Terri said, "but I'd appreciate it if you'd limit your questions to our jewelry."

I nodded. "Okay, I'll ask you something about the shop. Exactly who inherits it now that your father's gone? Is it a fifty-fifty split, or was one of you favored over the other? Do you have any idea what that might be worth? And what about Linda Mae? Does her presence here change anything? Was she mentioned in the will at all? Do you expect a fight from her?" I turned to Andrew and added, "Did your dad give you an even share, or did you get shafted in the will?"

Andrew started toward me, and I stood my ground. I'd been trying to make him mad with that last jab, hoping he would let something slip. Unfortunately, I think I may have pushed him a little too hard. There had been tension brewing between the two of us for twenty years, and while I never went looking for a fight in my life, if he took a swing at me it would be all the invitation I needed.

ƎIGHT

○ ○ ○

TERRI stepped quickly between us before anything could happen. "Honestly, you two are acting just like children. Ben, I need to ask you to leave."

I thought about turning her request down, but I wasn't going to uncover anything if I got into a fight with one of my suspects. I backed up as I said, "Sorry, I didn't mean to imply anything. I was just curious."

I walked out, got in the Miata, and drove around the block before finding a good parking place where I could keep an eye on the jewelry shop without being seen. The Joys were clearly hiding something, and I was determined to find out exactly what they were up to. I planned to follow whoever left the shop first to see if I could find a lead, but my Miata was a little too conspicuous on the streets of Harper's Landing. I drove back to the soap shop and approached my mother.

"I need to talk to you."

There was a look of concern in her eyes as she asked, "Ben, what is it?"

"First, I need to know if anyone has heard from Paulus lately."

"Why? What's wrong, Ben?" Though I knew the two of them had their share of problems, I also knew the love they'd felt for my father was a strong bond between them.

"Maybe nothing, but I'm a little worried about him. We were supposed to meet earlier and he never showed up."

Mom waved a hand in the air. "Your grandfather is not the most reliable man in the world," she said. "He probably got distracted. You know how he is."

"Maybe," I said, though I didn't believe it for a second.

"So what's second? You said first, now I'm waiting to hear what comes next."

"I need to trade vehicles with you. What do you say? You can drive the Miata, and I'll take your minivan."

She shook her head. "No thank you. I like to drive a grown-up's vehicle. It's high time you started driving one yourself."

"Mom, I'm not asking you to go for a joyride. I'm digging into Earnest Joy's murder, and my car stands out just a little too much. This is for the family." They were magic words with my mother. To her, family was everything.

"Take it," she said, digging into her apron pocket and producing her car keys.

"Thanks," I said as I tried to hand her the keys to my Miata. "Keep them, Benjamin, you might need them later."

"I don't want to leave you stranded," I said.

Mom laughed. "With all these children here dying to give their mother a ride? Don't be silly."

I kissed her on the cheek. "Thanks. I don't know when I'll have it back to you."

"I'll expect to get it back when I see you handing me the keys. Benjamin, be careful."

"Always," I said as I hurried for the door. I needed to get back and start my surveillance of the jewelry shop. At least in my Mom's gray minivan, I'd have a chance to blend into the surroundings. The vehicle was roomy, and the seat more comfortable than my Miata's, but it was going to be a bear to park, and I didn't look forward to topping off my mother's gas tank when I was finished with it.

I got back to the Joys just in time to see an intense-looking man getting into a white-paneled van, a black case grasped firmly in his left hand. I don't know what caused my instant suspicion of him. Maybe it was the way he scanned the streets before he got into his vehicle, as if he were searching for someone like me watching him. Even with my mother's tinted windows, I still ducked down in my seat when his gaze swept past me. As he drove off, I saw the lettering on the side of his van. In scripted letters, it said, Davis Fine Jewelry. He was probably just a regular supplier of theirs. So why had he acted so oddly?

I was still wondering about it when I saw Terri come out of the shop. Though my money was on Andrew as the chief suspect, I knew that Terri no doubt stood to inherit as well, giving her motive enough to kill her father and try to frame someone in the Perkins clan.

It was time to see what Terri Joy was up to.

I followed her to the outskirts of town, wondering what could possibly bring her there. When she pulled into the parking lot of the Mountain Lake Motel, I tucked the mini-van into a spot ten slots from her car. The rooms all had outside doors, and if Terri was going into a room close enough to where she was parked, I might just be able to see who she was visiting.

Without any hesitation, she knocked on one of the doors, waited a minute, then tried again. Her hostess was dressed in a robe with a white towel wrapped around her head, but I could still easily recognize her. It was Linda Mae. If Terri disliked her stepmother as much as she'd claimed, what was she doing visiting her? They both disappeared inside the room, and I debated whether to head back to trail Andrew when he left or wait it out. After ten minutes, I was growing impatient, and I started the minivan. As I did, Linda Mae's door opened and Terri came out. Her face was flushed, and she looked upset about something.

As she drove back to town, I tailed her, but she'd looked so upset that I could have been driving a fire truck and I don't think she would have noticed. I half expected her to head back to the jewelry store; but instead, she went directly to a small apartment complex and pulled into a spot near the pool. After she disappeared inside one of the units, I had to get a closer look to see who she was visiting this time. I casually got out of the minivan and walked past her door. Her name was printed near the buzzer. So Terri had gone straight home after going to see her stepmother.

I had just finished reading her name when I heard a woman's voice behind me. How in the world was I going to explain my presence there?

"Can I help you?" she asked. For a second I was sure it was Terri, but when I turned around, I found a lean blonde in a tailored business suit standing there.

"I'm at the wrong apartment," I said, backing away from Terri's door.

I was four steps away when she said, "Tell me who you're looking for. I know everyone at Sunny Side."

The problem was that I didn't know anybody there. Inspiration suddenly struck. "This is Sunny Side?" I said. "I'm looking for Henderson Place."

She frowned at me. "That's on the other side of town. How in the world did you end up here?"

"Bad directions, I guess. Thanks for your help."

"But I didn't do anything," she said as I hurried to Mom's minivan.

I drove off as fast as I could, but when I checked my rearview mirror, the woman was still staring after me.

As I raced back to the jewelry shop, I hoped Andrew was still there. I would have loved to know what Terri and Linda Mae had talked about, especially what had gotten Terri so upset when she drove off. If she disliked her stepmother that much, why had she driven straight to her motel room after talking to me? For that matter, how had she even known where she was? I needed to dig into that more. It could be tied to Earnest Joy's murder.

Andrew's car, a Mustang from the seventies in dire need of a paint job, was still parked in front of the jewelry store when I got back. The minivan was a great deal more comfortable than my Miata, especially for extended surveillance. I moved to the middle row of seats so I could stretch my legs out and was just settling in for a long wait when Andrew came out. Without even bothering to flip their OPEN sign to CLOSED, he locked the store up and got into his car. I scrambled forward and was barely buckled in by the time he ripped past me. Maybe I'd been rash swapping vehicles with my Mother. Andrew wouldn't stand a chance losing me if I'd been in my car, but I wasn't sure if the minivan could keep up with him. As I hurried through the streets of Harper's Landing, I hoped Molly wasn't out on patrol. I didn't want to have to explain why I was tailing Andrew Joy around town, especially while driving my mother's car. She'd probably lock me up on general principle.

In five minutes, Andrew pulled up in the driveway of his father's house. I thought about how I could get a better look inside when he surprised me and bypassed his dad's door, instead cutting across the lawn to Ralph's house. There was no place I could park on the street without being noticed, so I drove down the block as slowly as I could, trying not to wreck as I watched Andrew as he approached the front door. I saw Ralph open it before Andrew even had time to knock. It was almost as if he'd been waiting for his guest to show up. Ralph and Andrew both stepped quickly inside, and I nearly hit a Hummer parked in the street. The thing was as big as a school bus, and I hadn't been watching very closely. I circled the block a couple of times, then headed back to the soap shop. As far as I knew, I was finished tailing people for the day, and I wanted my Miata back.

I walked back in and Cindy shoved a note in my hand. "Special delivery," she said.

"What's this?" I asked.

"Open it and find out."

I tucked it in my shirt pocket. "I'll read it later. So how did class go? Did Kate help you?"

Cindy beamed. "She didn't have to. I did it all myself. You know what? I'm going to sign up for the next class myself."

I loved the smile on my youngest sister's face. "Cindy, I don't think you need to take a class. You're already pretty good at soapmaking. If you need a refresher, I'd be happy to help you out myself."

"Benjamin Perkins, I'm talking about signing up to teach, and you know it." She paused, then added, "You know what? You were right. I had fun."

"I'm sorry," I said, cupping a hand behind my ear. "What did you say? I missed it."

"I said I had fun."

I shook my head. "No, that wasn't it. You said something about me."

She laughed. "Okay, you win. You were right, and I was wrong. Happy now?"

"It's a good start," I said as Kate and Louisa joined us. Kate said, "What are you two chattering about?"

"Cindy's got the teaching bug," I said.

Kate nodded. "She should. She's better at it than you are."

"Hey, that's not fair," Louisa said, apparently in my defense.

Kate looked at her and said, "I didn't say she was better than you. Just Ben. You know how clumsy our oldest brother can be."

Louisa pretended to consider it. "He does tend to bang around into things, doesn't he?"

I shook my head. "You three should at least have the decency to do this when I'm not around. By the way, has anyone heard from Paulus?"

That effectively killed their jovial moods. When they all admitted that they hadn't, I said, "I'll be in my office if anybody needs me. I've got some phone calls to make."

Jeff was absent in back as Bob and Jim struggled with a heavy batch of soap they were preparing to pour. "Do you two need a hand?"

"We've got it," Bob said, though they were clearly struggling with the weight of the container.

Ignoring him, I grabbed an edge and helped them move it to the finishing line.

Jim wiped his forehead when we had it in place. "Thanks. That was a little heavier than I thought it would be."

"Where's Jeff?" I asked, looking around the production area.

Bob wouldn't answer, so Jim finally said, "He's not back from lunch yet."

I looked at my watch and saw that nearly three hours had passed since he'd left. "You're kidding, right? Since when did we start taking extended lunch hours?"

"Don't say anything to him," Bob said.

Jim added, "Yeah, we've already planned our lecture. He's going to wish he'd scrubbed with lye soap by the time we're through with him."

"Take it easy on him, guys. He's in love."

Neither one of them knew how to take that, especially coming from me.

Bob asked, "You have any luck finding Grandpa?"

"Not yet," I said. "Have you been talking to our sisters?"

Jim smiled. "Try to avoid them. They've been pestering us to go out and help you look, like we don't have three orders we're behind on already." He put the rag down he'd been wiping his hands with and added, "We will, you know. Help you look for him. Just say the word."

Bob nodded. "Family comes first."

"Thanks, but I'm still not completely convinced he didn't just bug out on me."

Jim said, "We're just saying. Let us know if you change your mind."

"You two will be the first ones I ask." I headed upstairs to my office, wanting to be alone with my thoughts for a little while.

I wasn't sure how long I sat there trying to figure out what my grandfather had stumbled into, and where he was right now. It was exactly like Paulus to take off without telling anyone, and if he hadn't called me and insisted on meeting me at The Hound Dog, I would have just passed it off as one of his flights of fancy. As it stood, though, I knew something had happened to keep him from meeting me. The real question in my mind was whether his recent paranoia was justified. I knew better than anyone how investigating a murder could make you constantly look over your shoulder for the bad guys. Had the same thing happened to Paulus, or had he actually stumbled onto a clue? If he'd tipped his hand to the murderer, I knew he could be in serious trouble. I picked up the phone, started to call Molly, then thought better of it. I had to have more proof than a skipped lunch if I was going to convince her that something might have happened to him. I made a few calls instead, but no one had seen Paulus all day.

It was time for drastic action. I knew how my grandfather felt about his privacy, and none of us were invited to his home except for special occasions. But it was time to snoop around his place to see if I could find anything that might tell me what he'd been up to, and what had thrown him into such a panic.

It took me ten minutes to drive to Paulus's house, but it was another fifteen before I got up the nerve to approach the front door. He lived in a large, rambling old place that needed a new roof and a good coat of paint. I'd once asked him why he hadn't fixed it up, and he'd told me that the house was a lot like he was: seasoned and experienced, without the need or desire to be something it wasn't. His response had been a little too esoteric for my tastes, but then that was Paulus through and through.

I knew there were half a dozen keys hidden around the property, since Paulus was notorious for misplacing them. He'd stash one somewhere, forget where it was, then repeat the process until his place was an invitation to a burglar, though from the looks of it on the outside, any self-respecting thief would pass it by. Maybe there was a good reason for its lack of curb appeal after all.

I checked under the mat, in the mailbox, and on the top door frame, but there weren't any keys there. Maybe Paulus had changed his habits, but I doubted it. Most likely it just meant that I'd have to search a little harder.

I finally found a key hiding under a whimsical elf that sat on the railing of his porch. Making a silent request for forgiveness from my grandfather, I used the key and slipped inside. The place was neat, and in surprising contrast to the exterior had been decorated tastefully with antiques. The hardwood floors were polished to a blinding shine, and the scent of lemons was everywhere, no doubt from the furniture polish my grandfather loved to use. I walked through the house, searching for something that might help me find him—or at the very least figure out what he'd been up to—when I spotted a note on the kitchen table.

To my surprise, it was addressed to me.

What was that about? I opened it and read, *Hi, Ben. You just couldn't resist snooping around my place, could you? That's a bad habit you've got there, sticking your nose in other people's business. I'm sorry about lunch—I should have come—but I got skittish at the last minute, came back here to pack a bag, and the second I'm finished with this, I'm getting out of town.*

Take my advice and drop it, Ben. Molly's on top of things, and she's good at her job. So let her do it. She knows how to get in touch with me when this mess is settled. In the meantime, I'm taking a trip I've been dreaming about for quite a while now.

Concentrate on what's real and what's not. That's the most important advice I can give you. Paulus.

What in blazes did that mean? Had my grandfather finally slipped off the edge of the dock of sanity? And what about that ringing endorsement of Molly? He could tell her where he was, but none of us? Then I remembered wheedling his last known whereabouts out of Kate, and realized he probably was right.

I couldn't just leave it at that, though, not with my neck on the block. It was time to talk to Molly.

I locked the house back up, stepped out onto the porch, and dialed her cell phone number.

I was beginning to wonder if she was even going to pick up when she said breathlessly, "Wilkes."

"Hey, Molly, it's Ben. We need to talk."

I could hear a sigh, then she said, "This isn't a good time."

"I'll bet," I said, "but I need to speak with you, anyway. Where's Paulus?"

"I'm not getting into this with you right now," she said.

"Don't hang up. If you do, I'll just keep calling, and I know you can't turn your phone off. Where is he?"

"Out of Harper's Landing," she said. "That's all you need to know. I've got to go."

"Why, are you on a big date?"

"As a matter of fact, I am."

"Sorry. I didn't know. Tell Jeff I didn't mean to interrupt your afternoon off."

There was a short bark of laughter. "I don't think so. Good-bye."

She didn't even wait for me to say good-bye myself. What was there left for me to do at the moment? It was close enough to closing time that I didn't see any need to go back to the soap shop, especially when I didn't have any answers to the questions I would surely get from my family. I wasn't in any hurry to go to my apartment, either.

Most times I enjoyed living by myself, but sometimes it was lonelier than I'd ever admit to anybody else.

I drove downtown, got a sandwich and drink to go from a sub shop, and headed to Bartholomew Grant's secret garden. It would be the perfect place to have a picnic for one.

When I got there, though, the lights were already on. Bartholomew, or another member of his inner circle, was visiting the garden. Kept behind a gate and tall hedge, the rest of the world was mostly ignorant to the spectacular flower garden he kept improving in honor of his late wife Leah. Since that option was gone, and I didn't feel like driving out to the dam, I decided to eat in the Miata right there. After I finished my meal, it was still too early to go home, and I found myself driving to Diana's bookstore. I'd missed seeing her today in class, and she was exactly the kind of company I was in the mood for tonight. Maybe she could even recommend a new author to me. I was always on the lookout for fresh talent.

The store was crowded when I walked in, and Rufus, her ponytailed clerk, was busy helping customers. He nodded to me, and when there was a gap in his line, I asked, "Is Diana around?"

"No, sorry, she's off tonight. Again." Another customer approached, and Rufus started ringing up his purchase. I browsed for a few minutes, then left without buying anything. As I drove back to my apartment, I couldn't help wondering where Diana was. Out on another date, perhaps? It was none of my business—we'd only gone out once—but I still felt a twinge of jealousy.

By the time I got to my place, I was in a dark mood. Maybe a movie and some microwave popcorn would help. I sat through the opening of *The Godfather*, flipped it off and grabbed a book, but I quickly put it back down. I just wasn't in the mood to be entertained.

As I undressed and got ready for bed, I felt a slip of paper in my pocket. I'd forgotten all about the note Cindy had given me.

I took it out and saw that it was from Diana. This was my day to get correspondence.

> *Ben, sorry I missed you today. If you'd like to call me tonight, go ahead, no matter how late it is. I'm visiting my aunt and uncle in Hunter's Hollow tonight, but I'll be back around ten.*
> *Diana.*
> *PS I had a wonderful time last night. Thanks again for asking.*

I glanced at the clock and saw that it was a little before ten. Should I call her, or wait until my mood wasn't quite so dark? Finally, I decided talking to her might just be the exact thing I needed.

She answered before it even had the chance to ring twice. "Hello?"

"I just got your note," I said. "How were your aunt and uncle?"

"Ben," she said happily, the delight obvious in her voice. "I was hoping you'd call. They're fine. My uncle is building a boat in the basement, and he's just about finished. There's just one problem."

"What's that?" I asked.

"It's too big to get through the door." Her laughter was delightful, and I found my mood starting to lighten.

"Is he devastated?"

"You'd think so, wouldn't you? He's looking at it as a challenge, and knowing my uncle, he'll figure something out. When I left, he was trying to talk my aunt into letting him put hinges on the house so he could just lift it up. They are absolutely hilarious. So how was your day? I missed you in class."

"Sorry about that. I had to take care of some family business."

She hesitated, then said, "Listen, this may be out of line, and if it is just tell me, but if you need some help looking into Earnest Joy's murder, I'm right here. I've been reading mysteries my entire life, and I've gotten pretty good at figuring them out."

"I wish it were that simple," I said. "I appreciate the offer, but I don't even know where to begin."

"That's fine, but I'm here if you need me. Ben, it's so nice to hear your voice."

"It's good hearing yours, too." And it was. My mood had lifted considerably just listening to her tales of her family. We talked for nearly an hour before saying our good-byes, and I didn't have a single problem getting to sleep after our conversation.

It was good having Diana in my life, and I'd thought of Kelly only a few times that day. Maybe I was going to be able to move on, after all.

NINE

o o o

I was at The Hound Dog the next morning eating my breakfast before work when I glanced over my shoulder and saw Ralph Haller come in. The last time I'd spoken to the man, he'd accused me of murder and had nearly come after me, even with Molly standing beside me.

I ducked down in my booth and listened to his footsteps approach. Had he seen me? I braced myself for another confrontation when I heard him say nearly in my ear, "How are you doing, you wretched piece of garbage?"

I was starting to stand up when another voice said, "Look who's talking? At least I've never been in prison."

"Not that you didn't deserve it a time or two," Ralph said as he slid into the booth directly behind me.

The other man said, "Deserving's one thing, but doing the time's another."

"That's ancient history, McGregor. What looks good today?"

"Ruby's sporting a new hairdo," his companion said.

"I'm talking about food, you tire iron. Tell you what. Order me a stack of pancakes and some eggs. I've got to hit the can."

"You're a charmer, Ralph, you know that, don't you?"

I waited until I heard Ralph's footsteps retreat to the restroom, then I took off, leaving half my meal still on my plate. I threw a ten to Ruby and left before Ralph came back out and saw me.

Once I was back at Where There's Soap, I started wondering about the conversation the two men had shared. Could it be true that Ralph had spent time in prison? I wondered what he'd been convicted of. Maybe murder, or aggravated assault. Could he have killed Earnest Joy, then planted the soap in his left hand to divert Molly's attention toward the Perkins clan? I had to know. I thought about calling Molly, but her scolding the afternoon before still stung, and I wasn't in the mood to get another lecture at the moment. If I found something a little more concrete I'd go to her, but not until then.

It was a miracle that nobody bothered me in my office all morning. I waited around until the library was open, then left as quickly as I could. It was time to dig into the past. If Paulus had been around I would have asked him, but as it was, I was going to have to do my research the old-fashioned way.

"I need some help," I asked the librarian behind the reference desk. She was a petite red-haired woman with a quick smile and a ready laugh. Her nametag read, Corki.

"That's why I'm here," she said. "What are you looking for?"

"I've got a man's name and a rumor that he went to prison a long time ago, and I need to know what happened to send him there. His name's Ralph Haller. The only problem is, I'm not sure when he was convicted, except that it was sometime thirty or forty years ago."

Corki smiled quickly. "I love a challenge first thing in the morning. Let's see, I'll start you on the microfilm of our newspaper archives while I make a few phone calls."

"I don't want to be a bother," I said.

"Please," she said. "This is my idea of fun."

"Then you need to get out more," I said.

"Is that an invitation or a general observation? I'm a married woman, you know."

I stammered, "Well, it's not that I . . . I mean . . ."

She watched me squirm a moment longer, then said, "I'm just teasing. Before you start digging, let's try something else first."

Corki leaned into her terminal and started typing at a fierce pace. Every now and then she'd nod, pause, then tap a few more keys. "Okay, here's what I've found so far. There's no Ralph Haller on the Internet listings for convictions in North Carolina in the time frame you're talking about."

"Sorry I wasted your time," I said as I started to leave.

"Hold on a second. You don't truly believe I'm going to give up that easily, do you? I did an alternate search for Ralph H convictions, and I've got five possibilities for you." She handed me a sheet with five dates printed on it. "You can check the newspaper stories while I keep digging."

She led me to a corner where the microfilm was stored, along with two ancient viewers. "I'm afraid you'll have to search by hand. This system is antiquated, but it's the best we can do with our budget."

"This is fine," I said.

"Do you know how to work the machine?"

I nodded. "Back when I went to college, this was state of the art."

"You wouldn't believe how hard it is to teach the kids how to use this equipment. If you find anything before I do, come tell me."

"Thanks again," I said as she stacked four reels of film on the desk.

"I haven't even gotten started yet," she said.

I threaded the filmstrip through the viewer, then flipped on the lamp. Only then did I realize that I'd put it in upside down and backwards. Quickly correcting my mistake, I started scrolling through the dates until I got to the first entry. It was the wrong Ralph, as well as the next one, but on my third try, I found him. Age hadn't been a friend to him over the years, but there was no mistaking that chin and prominent nose of his. I scanned the article until I found what I was looking for.

Ralph Haliford—not Ralph Haller as he was going by now—had been convicted thirty years ago. I held my breath as I scanned the article, hoping it would show something that dovetailed into Earnest Joy's murder. No such luck. Haliford had been an inept burglar, getting himself caught in the mayor's house with a bag of stolen swag. As far as I could tell, it was another dead end.

Just to have a record of it, I fed the machine a quarter and hit the PRINT button, but all I got was a black image on the paper.

Corki came up behind me. "Sorry, it's broken. But I found something else you might be interested in."

"Thanks anyway, but I have just what I need."

I started to take the tape out of the machine when she said, "Go ahead, I'll take care of this."

"I appreciate it."

She shrugged. "Why not? It's quiet right now, and I'd rather stay busy than get bored."

I left the library, wondering what to do next. Ralph might be an ex-con, but that didn't automatically make him a murderer. Still, I wondered if Molly knew about his record. I thought about calling her, but our last conversation hadn't gone very well, and I wasn't really looking forward to getting spanked again. I'd just have to take it, though. She needed to know.

"Wilkes," she said when she answered her phone.

"Hey, it's Ben," I said.

Her voice was chilled as she said, "What do you want?"

"First off, I'd like to apologize."

She paused, then said, "Go on, you've got my attention. What are you apologizing for?"

"It's about yesterday. I'm sorry I interrupted your date. It was purely unintentional. I hope you know that."

"Is that it?" she asked, clearly not satisfied with the level of my remorse.

"For the apology, yes. There's something else, though."

"Now how did I know there would be?"

Boy, she surely wasn't making this any easier on me. "Did you know that Earnest Joy's neighbor, Ralph Haller, is really Ralph Haliford, and that the reason he's living under an assumed name is because he served time in prison?"

"Ben, I swear you are relentless. When you said you called to apologize, I thought it might be for sticking your nose in where it didn't belong."

"Hardly," I said. "Did you know about Haller?"

She snapped, "Of course I knew. He served his time, came back here, and changed his name legally to Haller. If you think he killed Earnest Joy, you're wrong. He's got an alibi I'm satisfied with. Ben, believe it or not, I do know what I'm doing. I just wish I could say the same thing for you."

"That's not fair. You've got a lot more resources than I do. How am I supposed to compete with that?"

"You're not," she said, then hung up on me. Okay, that exchange could have gone better. Not only was Molly aware of Haller's record, she'd already checked out his alibi.

So who else could I investigate? No doubt Molly had tested Andrew's and Terri's alibis, but did she even know about Linda Mae? I couldn't exactly call and ask her at the moment, but I could dig into that angle without alerting Molly.

I drove to the Mountain Lake Motel, found the room Terri had visited the afternoon before, and knocked on the door. Linda Mae answered dressed in a bathrobe and her hair wrapped up in a white towel. Did the woman ever wear clothes in her room?

She had her wallet in her right hand as she said, "It's about time," then she realized it was me. "Why Ben Perkins, how did you know I was here?"

"I'd like to talk to you, Linda Mae."

She stepped aside. "I was waiting for some Chinese takeout. There's enough for both of us; I always order too much."

"Would you like to get dressed first?" I asked. A fully clothed Linda Mae was enough to deal with.

She clapped her hands. "You are just the sweetest thing. If you insist, I'll need a minute. You can come in and wait while I get dressed, if you want to."

"No, thanks," I said.

She was laughing as she shut her door. While I was waiting, a college kid drove up in a beat-up old Chevrolet.

He checked room numbers, then looked at me suspiciously. "Did you have an order from Pete's Palace?"

"I'll take it," I said, reaching into my wallet and paying the bill myself.

After he was gone, Linda Mae threw the door back open. She was wearing a tight black sweater and snug Capri pants, doing her best to show off her figure.

When she spotted the bag in my hands, she asked, "Did he come by already?"

"He did," I said as I stepped inside.

"Here, let me pay you for that," she said, digging into her wallet.

"I'll buy your lunch if you answer a few questions," I said.

Linda Mae clapped her hands. "If you pay for my meal, you're entitled to more than that."

"Answers are all I'm looking for right now," I said.

She shrugged. "That's probably just as well. You've got a woman in your life already, don't you? Don't bother denying it, I can see it in your eyes."

In all honesty, I didn't know the answer to that question myself. "Let's just say I've got all I can handle as it is right now and leave it at that, okay?"

"That's fine by me," she said, extending her hand. "Then we'll both have to settle for just being friends."

I wasn't sure I wanted this woman as a friend, but I wasn't about to snub her. I shook her hand, then she pointed to the small table in the room. "See? I already set the table." The room, though not elegant by any standard, did have a kitchenette. Linda Mae had laid out the plates and silverware, along with a pair of beers from her mini fridge.

I hadn't realized I was hungry until I'd smelled that

food. Suddenly my skipped lunch made my stomach growl. "Are you sure you have enough to share?"

"There's plenty. Believe me. Besides, you're the one sharing with me, remember?"

"Okay," I said.

We dug into the assorted containers until our plates were full.

"You weren't kidding, were you?" I asked as I realized just how much she'd ordered.

"I never joke about food, Ben. I always get more than I want when I'm out of town. That way if I get hungry late at night, I don't have to go out again. You said you had some questions for me," she said as she pointed her chopsticks at me. "Fire away."

I swallowed a bite, then said, "Tell me about you and Earnest."

She thought about it a second, then said, "To most of the world he was a cold, heartless man, but for a while there, I saw a side to him that really touched me. Earnest came to Charlotte on a buying trip and we ran into each other at a pawn shop. He was looking for old coins for his jewelry shop, and unfortunately, I was there selling my grand-mother's pearl earrings. The man wooed me for nine days with flowers, candy, and gifts. He catered to my every whim, and even flew me to Las Vegas to see a show. That night we both got drunk, and when I woke up the next morning, there was a ring on my finger. I don't know how he managed it, but we got married. Man, oh man, did things change then. That afternoon, Ernie handed me a ticket to Charlotte and told me he was going back to Harper's Landing, and that I wasn't welcome to join him."

I believed her, every word of it, but I had a hard time

seeing Earnest Joy in that light. "So what did you do then?"

She took another bite, then followed it up with a sip of beer. "I flew back home and cried in my cups, trying to forget that it had ever happened. Then one day last week I was messing around on my computer and decided to see what I could find out about my errant husband. When I discovered he had his own jewelry store and everything, I drove up here to have a little talk with him."

"Were you hoping to reconcile?" I asked her.

Linda Mae laughed. "No sir, I was after a little divorce settlement. When I came by his shop, he threw me out. I wasn't about to give up that easily though, so I came back the next day and found out he was dead. That's when I marched over to your soap shop and shook your hand. Are you still claiming you didn't do it?"

"It's the truth," I said.

"Take it easy. I'm not accusing you of anything. You might just be right, since you're still walking around. I wonder if one of those brats of his did him in."

"Do you know Andrew and Terri very well?" I still hadn't told Linda Mae how I'd found her, and it appeared that she'd forgotten she'd asked the question.

"No, we never met. I doubt I could pick either one of them out of a lineup."

She was the best liar I'd ever come across. I'd seen Terri go into her room, and she was sitting there now telling me they'd never met. Suddenly everything she said was suspect.

"So what are you going to do now?" I asked.

"I'm going to see how much I get from the estate," she said. "One way or another, Ernie's going to pay."

"They won't settle until they find out who killed him,

you know," I said. I wasn't sure if they would or not, but I was looking for some kind of reaction from her.

"That shouldn't take too long," she said. "I've got faith in your police force." She pushed her plate away, then stood. "That was lots of fun, Ben, but I'm late for an appointment."

As she walked me to the door, I said, "I didn't think you knew anybody in Harper's Landing."

"What can I say, I make friends fast."

She locked her door behind us, then got into a Cadillac that was at least fifteen years old. "See you around, Ben."

I waited until she was gone, then got into my Miata and followed her. I was expecting her to go to a bar or even another motel. I did not expect her to do what she did. Linda Mae pulled the Caddy in front of Kelly Sheer's office and walked inside. It appeared that she was retaining counsel in Harper's Landing. But could she afford Kelly? I didn't see how, given the apparent state of her finances, but perhaps she was hoping Kelly would take her on a contingency basis. I thought about waiting until she came out to see where she was going next, but sitting in front of Kelly's law office was not my favorite place to be. I looked at my watch and was surprised to see that Kelly was working late, given her new living arrangements. Was there trouble already? If there was, I realized it wasn't any of my business anymore.

I was close enough to visit Diana's bookstore, but I didn't want her to think I was stalking her. Still, it wouldn't hurt to drive by. She was working in the display window as I neared, and she waved at me. That was all the invitation I needed. I parked in front of Dying To Read and she met me at the front door.

"Do you always hang out in your display window?" I asked.

"We're doing an author signing next month, and I want

to give everyone fair warning." She lowered her voice and added, "I'm having second thoughts about it. I spoke with another store owner and found out the woman's a real nightmare."

"What's wrong, does she demand all the brown M&M's be taken out of her candy bowl?"

"I wish it were that simple," Diana said. "When her publicist called to book the signing, I was thrilled, but I got an e-mail from her today, and she's made the most unusual request."

"I'm really curious now. What did she ask for?"

Diana looked around the store to make sure no one was listening to us. I saw Rufus had his head buried in a book, and there were just a few customers browsing the cozy section. She whispered, "She insists that her books not be referred to as mysteries while she's here. Ben, I run a mystery bookstore. How on earth am I going to avoid it?"

I shook my head. "Beats me. Suddenly I'm very glad I'm in the soapmaking business."

Diana laughed. "Don't get me wrong, nearly all the authors I bring in are delightful, but sometimes I wonder why I do it. Then I remember that it's fun for my customers to meet their favorites, and they often buy lots of books."

"How about you? Have you met any of your literary heroes?"

She pointed to one of an array of photographs hanging near the register. "That's me with Carolyn Hart. She's as warm and as gracious as her characters. What an utterly delightful woman."

"Are all of these photographs on display new?" I asked as I pointed to several frames I'd never noticed before.

"I just put them up today," she admitted. "There wasn't room enough in my office, so I decided to mount them out here where everyone can enjoy them. I feel a little odd about it all, since I'm in every picture."

"That's what makes them special," I said. As soon as I said it, I realized how it must have sounded. The groan from Rufus didn't help matters.

"I'm going on my dinner break," he said as he brushed past me.

"Don't stay too long," Diana said, but he was already gone. She moved behind the register, then asked, "Have you eaten yet, Ben? I'd be delighted to return the favor and take you out. We even have time to go to The Hound Dog."

"I'll keep you company," I said, "but I grabbed an early bite."

"We'll do it another time then," she said. "I brought a salad from home, anyway."

A male customer came up and asked, "Can you help me? Somebody told me Donald Westlake was writing under another name, but I can't remember for the life of me what he said."

"Mr. Westlake's written under several different names, but I suspect you want Richard Stark."

The man said, "Yeah, the guy's name is Tucker, or something like that, right?"

"It's Parker," she said with a smile. "Let me show you."

I said, "I'll see you later, Diana."

"Bye, Ben. Thanks for stopping by."

I left the shop feeling good. Diana had a way of making me feel important to her day in a way that I really liked. Though Kelly was still in my thoughts sometimes, I knew that I was doing the right thing moving on.

I was still thinking about the extraordinary changes in my life over the past few days when I literally bumped into Terri Joy out on the street.

"Hey, slow down," I said as she hustled past me.

There was a look of fear in her eyes as she saw me. "Ben, I think somebody's following me."

I looked up and down the block, but I didn't see anyone paying particular attention to us.

"What makes you say that?"

She pointed to a mass of people standing around the Blake Theater. "He's right there." As she stared at the crowd, she added, "At least he was."

"Take it easy, Terri. Why would anyone be following you?" It was an ironic question for me to be asking her, since I'd followed her myself before.

"How should I know?" she snapped. After a moment's hesitation, she added, "I bet Linda Mae's doing it. She's got some deluded idea that she and my father were really married, but until I see a wedding license, I'm not about to believe it."

"She obviously knew your dad though, didn't she?"

Terri shrugged. "So what? He had a fling with her. He was a grown man, I suppose he was entitled. But I know he never would have married her. It wasn't anything he'd ever do."

"Sometimes people do things out of character," I said.

"Come on, Ben," she said as she looked into my eyes. "You knew my father and you've met Linda Mae. Can you possibly imagine them as a couple?"

"Who's to say what the heart wants," I said. "If you'd like, I'd be happy to walk you to your car."

She glanced back at the group waiting to get into the theater. "Thanks, but it looks like he's gone. You must have scared him off."

Before I could ask her anything else, she was gone. What was that about? I'd been counting Terri among my list of suspects, but it sounded as though she might be in jeopardy herself. Why would someone follow her, anyway? Was it possible she knew something important that she wasn't aware of? She and her brother Andrew were still my main suspects, but Ralph and Linda Mae might have also had their reasons to want Earnest dead. Too, there could be someone else out there that I didn't know about, but if that were the case, I might as well give up. Molly had the resources and the expertise to dig into Earnest Joy's life. I could focus on the four people I knew were suspects. Of course Molly had me on her list too—as well as the rest of my family in all likelihood—but I knew I was innocent, and my family as well. That gave me an edge over Molly. She had to be distracted by a surplus of suspects, while I could focus on just four people.

I decided I needed some time to think, so I got into the Miata and started driving in the direction of Sassafras Ridge. As I drove, I began to think about my suspects, and what their motives might have been. For Andrew and Terri, money had to be a factor. Earnest Joy's jewelry shop had to make a great deal of money, given the store's inventory and his taste for the nicer things in life. I couldn't imagine anyone killing a parent for an inheritance, but I knew people did it all the time, and given the right circumstances, I could see Andrew or Terri doing it. Linda Mae could have been concerned that Earnest would nullify their marriage— if they had indeed gotten married—so she might have killed him before he could disown her. Then again, she could have demanded a payoff to stay out of his life, and knowing Earnest, he would have probably laughed in her face. That blow to the head could have easily been done out of anger instead of greed. That left Ralph Haller. Why would he want Earnest dead? They were best friends from the sound of things, though he had to have had plenty of opportunity, but what about a motive? I needed to dig into that a little more and see what I could find out.

I turned the Miata around and decided to drive to Ralph's home. The last time I'd seen him he'd called me a murderer. Did I really want to go through that again? I didn't have much choice, but if I was going to try to solve Earnest's murder on my own, I needed to stand my ground.

Ralph's car was parked in his driveway. I walked up onto the porch, but before I knocked, I looked in through the side window next to the door. The curtain was askew, offering me a slight view inside his home. Ralph was sitting at the kitchen table with some rags, polishing something gold and shiny. I rapped on the door, and he quickly shoved whatever it was into a shoe box and tucked it under the sofa before answering my summons.

"What do you want?" he snapped the second he saw me.

"I need your help," I said. It was the first thing that popped into my mind.

"Why should I help you, Perkins?"

That was a good question, one I didn't have a ready answer for, except for the truth. "Don't you want to see that whoever killed Earnest is punished for it?"

"I know who killed him," he said. "I'm looking at him."

"I told you before; I didn't do it. And I don't think you did, either." That was a flat-out lie. He was still on my list of suspects, but I doubted he'd cooperate with me if he knew.

Ralph studied me a few seconds, then said, "What do you think you can do about it?"

Given his history, I came up with a way he might help. "Do you honestly believe the cops are going to figure it out?"

He looked at me like he wanted to spit. "They couldn't find a candy bar in a convenience store."

"So help me," I said.

He reluctantly nodded and stepped aside. Was I really doing the smartest thing in the world, grilling one of my suspects without a backup? No one even knew where I was. I realized that I should have at least checked in with someone, but it was too late for that. I stepped across the threshold, then he reached behind me and dead bolted the door.

"We don't want anybody sneaking up on us," he said.

"That's a good idea," I said as I started looking for another way out of there.

The place needed more than just a woman's touch. A Dumpster and a fire hose were the only things that might save it. Newspapers were piled up in the corners, and there were four old pizza boxes stacked up on the kitchen countertop. A thick layer of dust coated everything, and a stack of dirty dishes sat in the sink. I didn't even want to see the bedrooms or bathrooms if the public spaces were like that. I was going to try to sit on the sofa where he'd tucked that box, but he beat me to it. Instead, I took the armchair and faced him.

Before I could ask him anything, he said, "You really think you can figure this out on your own?"

"I've had a little luck doing it before," I said.

"What have you got so far?"

It was time to step a little lightly. "Well, we've got to consider the kids, no matter how unpleasant it is."

"Andrew loved his old man," Ralph said, "but Terri would have cut his throat for a dollar. I never trusted that kid, not from the second they brought her home from the hospital."

"Do you have anything to back that up?"

He looked at me as if I'd lost my mind. "We're not cops. We don't need proof. If you didn't do it, then I'm pretty sure she did."

"What makes you so sure about Andrew?"

Ralph growled as he said, "Leave the boy alone. I'm telling you, he loved his old man."

It was pretty obvious which child Ralph favored. "How about Linda Mae? She could have easily done it."

"That nut job?" Ralph asked. "She's as dumb as a brick if she thought Earnest loved her, let alone really married her."

"She called him Ernie," I said.

"There you go. He hated that name. You think he'd let that woman call him that? She's a nut job."

The telephone rang, and Ralph pounced on it.

"Yeah? Hang on." He covered the mouthpiece, then said, "We're finished, right?"

"There's a lot more I need to talk to you about. I don't mind waiting."

It was pretty obvious he wasn't interested in me hanging around. "I don't have anything left to say."

He walked to the front door, but I stayed put. "Molly Wilkes is going to ask me about this. We talk about everything. Wouldn't it be easier if I told her we'd already covered everything from your end of things? Otherwise she's going to keep nosing around here until she's satisfied." I was glad I wasn't wired to a polygraph. The needles would be dancing like Fred Astaire.

Ralph was still thinking about it when whoever was on the other end of the line started shouting. He said, "Keep your pants on." Then he looked at me and said, "I'll be right back."

The second he disappeared into the bedroom, I dove for the box stashed under the couch. Lying on top of a rag, half polished and half darkened with time, was a single gold coin. What was he doing with that? It appeared to be French, and pretty old. So why was Ralph polishing it? I heard the bedroom door open, so I tossed the coin back in and slid the lid in place.

As I shoved it under the couch, he said, "What do you think you're doing?"

"My shoe was untied," I said. And then I saw that I hadn't gotten the edge of the box all the way back under the sofa. As I stood, I started to move toward him so I could nudge it back in place.

"There are a few more things I'd like to ask you," I said, trying to find the box with my toe without him realizing what I was doing.

"Sorry, but we're finished here. I've got to go."

He took my arm and started walking me to the door. There was no way I could leave the box in a different place than where it belonged. I knocked a stack of magazines off a table near the door. "Sorry, I'm pretty clumsy."

"I'll get them later," he said, but his grip did lessen.

"Nonsense. I knocked them off, I'll restack them."

As I bent over to start picking them up, he got down on one knee to help, anything to get me out of there.

I put one magazine on top of the other and shot it toward the couch. "These things are slippery," I said as I reached for it. Before he could see what I was doing, I took the magazine's edge and shoved the box back under the couch. "Got it," I said.

"Come on, I'm late for an appointment," he said gruffly.

"I'll be by later then, so we can talk more."

He shook his head. "I'm done talking."

"Is that what I should tell Molly?"

"Tell her whatever you want to."

I opened the door and was surprised to find Andrew there getting ready to knock.

"What are you doing here?" he asked me with a snarl in

his voice. I looked down and saw that one hand was clenched around a section of gray pipe.

"Just visiting," I said. "What have you got there?" I asked as I gestured to the weapon.

"I'm not taking any chances since somebody killed my father. Let him try to sneak up on me." He patted the pipe in his open palm. "I'm ready."

"Good for you," I said as I slipped past him.

"Butt out, Perkins. This isn't any of your business, and I'd hate to see you get hurt."

The tone in his voice told me that he'd bring popcorn and soda if he knew I was going to get a beating.

"Yeah, I'd hate that, too." As I started to walk away, I turned back to him and said, "You know what? I'm not the only one who should be careful."

Andrew's face reddened in anger. "Are you threatening me? Ralph, you heard that. He just threatened me."

"Settle down, Andrew," Ralph said. "Come on inside."

"I'm not afraid of you," Andrew shouted at me.

"That's good, because you don't scare me, either. I'm not the one you have to watch out for, though."

His gaze narrowed. "What do you mean?"

"Nobody's killing Perkinses," I said.

"At least not yet," he said.

"Now who's making threats?"

Ralph grabbed Andrew's arm. "Get in here, and I mean right now."

I was ready for him, pipe and all, and it looked like he might come after me. Ralph jerked his arm again, though, and Andrew just smiled at me as he walked inside. "We'll finish this later."

"Any time," I said as I walked back to my car.

I half expected to see the Miata's windshield shattered,

but it was still intact as I got in and sped off. I wasn't quite sure where I was going, but I knew I wanted to get away from Ralph and Andrew. Once they started comparing notes about my behavior, I was afraid one or both of them were going to try to stop me from nosing around in their business. I wasn't excited about the prospect of looking over my shoulder all of the time, but I wasn't about to stop snooping.

Whether Molly or the rest of the world liked it, I wasn't about to stop until I found Earnest Joy's killer.

TEN

∘ ∘ ∘

SPEAK of the Devil and he appears. That's the way the old expression went, and it was true as I walked into Where There's Soap. Molly Wilkes, still dressed in her police uniform, was sitting on a rocking chair out front when I walked up the steps.

"You're here more than I am lately," I said. "Is this business or pleasure?"

"What do you think?" she asked.

"I'm not so sure anymore," I said.

"Have a seat, Ben. I've been waiting for you."

I took the rocker beside hers. "You haven't changed your mind about arresting me, have you?"

"Not unless you've changed your mind about confessing."

I laughed. "You know better than that. Why did you want to see me?"

"I just got a complaint about your behavior," she said. "And you're not going to believe who made it."

"I don't think I could narrow the field if I had to. Who have I offended lately?"

She smiled. "Andrew Joy called me twice today telling me you're interfering with my police investigation. That man seems to really enjoy hating you, doesn't he?"

"What can I say, I'm an acquired taste. We just had another confrontation, so expect your phone to be ringing in a few minutes."

She shook her head as she stared out at the garden. "You are determined to make this difficult for me, aren't you?"

"I'm not trying, I swear it," I said. "I just hate being your prime suspect."

Molly stared at me a second, then said, "If you repeat this to anyone, I'll deny it. Do we understand each other?"

"I know how to keep a secret," I said.

"That's why I'm telling you. Ben, don't be such a dunderhead. I know you didn't kill Earnest Joy."

"That's the best news I've heard all day. What changed your mind?"

She looked at me as she said, "If you were going to kill a man, even spur of the moment like that, you never would have hit him from behind. I know you. You'd have looked him in the eye as you killed him."

"Now why doesn't that explanation make me feel any better?" I asked.

"Sometimes the truth hurts." She rocked a few times, then asked, "Should I even ask about what you've been up to today?"

"No. Like you said, I'm good at keeping secrets."

As Molly started to get up, I asked, "Have you talked to Earnest's wife yet?"

"That's not remotely funny, Ben. Samantha Joy's been dead for fifteen years."

"I'm talking about his new wife. He got married a while ago in Vegas. At least that's what his bride is telling everybody in town."

Molly frowned. "She hasn't said anything to me. Where might I find this woman?"

"Her name's Linda Mae, and she's staying out at the Mountain Lake Motel. Room #23. Tell her I sent you, and she'll sing her head off."

"How long were you going to keep this to yourself? If she really was married to Earnest Joy, she could have an excellent reason for wanting him dead."

"Hey, I'm telling you right now," I said. "I just found out myself."

She got up and headed for her patrol car. "Do me a favor and tell Jeff I'll catch up with him later, okay?"

"Fine," I said. In twenty seconds, she was gone. Jeff walked out onto the porch as I was going in.

He looked around, then said, "Hey, what happened to Molly?"

"She had to go," I said, "but she asked me to tell you she'd talk to you later."

"What did you say to her, Ben?"

I was getting tired of that tone of voice, and I wasn't about to take it from my little brother anymore.

"Listen, if you want to be treated like a grown-up, why don't you start acting like one? I didn't say a word to her."

"I don't believe you."

"Frankly, I don't care."

I brushed past him, letting my arm hit his chest enough to stagger him back a step. It was time to remind him who the senior sibling was.

Cindy was standing by the door, not even pretending to be doing anything but eavesdropping.

She looked at me and said, "You're too big to pick on him like that."

"I wasn't doing anything," I protested.

"I saw what happened," Cindy said.

"Yeah, but you must not have heard any of it. Jeff needs to grow up."

She touched my arm. "Ben, why are you acting like that?"

I looked at her and said, "Cindy, I love you—you have to realize that—but you don't know everything about me. When I get pushed, I have a tendency to push back."

She looked at me sadly. "I know this has been hard on you."

"What's that, being a murder suspect?"

She shook her head. "I'm not talking about that, and you know it. I mean losing Kelly like you did and then watching your old girlfriend date your youngest brother."

"I'm seeing someone myself, remember?"

Cindy arched one eyebrow. "Are you that serious about Diana already? You two have just gone out on one date."

Blast it all, why did my siblings think it was all right to meddle in my life? "Kelly and I didn't have much more than that. Besides, I'm not ready to propose, but Diana and I are dating now. You know how I am. I've never been able to go out with more than one woman at a time, and right now, that woman is Diana." I looked around, and though Kate and Louisa were both helping customers, it was pretty obvious they were following every word of our discussion. "Did you all get that?" I asked.

Kate looked away, but Louisa just smiled. "Loud and clear. Benji's got a new girlfriend."

I shook my head, not dignifying her comment with a response. I'd hated the nickname "Benji" since kindergarten and had done everything in my power to discourage its usage.

I thought about going up to my office, but then realized the shop would be closing soon, and I didn't want to be there alone with my thoughts. I could call Diana, though it was short notice, but what I really needed to do was find Paulus and see what he'd found out that had made him run.

Where to look, though? He could be anywhere, and without access to his credit cards, I'd just have to guess.

Then I remembered where I'd found him the last time he'd been in hiding. I told my sisters good night and drove to Sassafras Ridge. As I drove, I realized Cindy was right. I'd been tougher on my little brother than I had the right to be. Lately, he found a way to get under my skin, but that was still no excuse for my behavior. I'd have to find a way to apologize the next time I saw him, but at the moment, I had to find Paulus. That took precedence over a family squabble.

I knew he wouldn't be at the Beverly. In fact, I doubted he'd choose his old motel room. But there was one thing I was fairly certain about. When it came to eating, Paulus was a man of entrenched habits. I knew that if hung out at the Lazy Spoon, sooner or later he'd turn up.

I was luckier than I deserved to be. Paulus was sitting in a booth in back eating a piece of apple pie.

There was no place he could bolt to, so he sat patiently in his seat as I approached him.

"Did anybody follow you here?" he asked me as he scanned the sidewalk.

"No, I made sure of it. Mind if I join you?" I asked as I slid onto the bench seat across from him.

"Do I have any choice?" he asked, then added a slight

smile. "I've got to hand it to you, Ben. You must really be some kind of detective, finding me like this."

"Don't give me too much credit," I said. "This was a logical place to look. You didn't go too far. So, do you want to talk to me now about what you uncovered?"

He stared at his pie, then said, "Ben, I told you to drop it, and I meant it. You got my note, didn't you?"

"You knew I would," I said. "Did you honestly think it would dissuade me?"

He shook his head. "No, but it was worth a shot. Ben, this is serious business."

"Murder always is," I said. "What's got you so spooked all of a sudden?"

He sighed. "Maybe I'm just getting old," he finally said. "I've lost a step or two, and a lot of the fire in my belly."

"Is that why you cleaned out your office?" I asked as the waitress filled the coffee mug in front of me.

I ordered myself a piece of pie. Paulus said, "I've been easing myself out of the business for a while now. Kate's been handling the advertising for years. The truth is, you all don't need me anymore."

The waitress put the pie on the table, but I didn't touch it. "That's just plain wrong. You're a part of our family."

He waved a hand in the air. "I know that, Benjamin, but I have to feel useful. That's why I started looking for other businesses. To be honest with you, that's kind of why I started digging into Earnest's murder, too. But I got myself in too deep, and look where that got me, hiding in a town I don't particularly care for in a diner that has aspirations of being average."

"Why don't you tell me about it?" I suggested. "If nothing else, I'm a good listener."

He seemed to think about it for nearly a minute before he spoke again. "Okay, why not? You're not going to stop—I know you—so you should at least know what you're dealing with."

"You've certainly got my attention," I said.

"I've long suspected Earnest Joy did more than sell jewelry at that shop of his. I started poking around, and I found out he's got a second home—a much nicer one, I might add—in Blowing Rock. That's where he keeps his fancy sports cars. The man's been hemorrhaging money for years. I had a friend check his tax returns for the past three years, and according to those, he barely makes a profit from his jewelry shop. So where's the money coming from?"

I had a hard time imagining the penurious Earnest Joy as a playboy, despite what Linda Mae had said. Blowing Rock was a ritzy community in the North Carolina mountains near Boone, and it was well known in our part of the world as a haven for the wealthy. "No offense, but how sure are you of your source?"

He took a sip of coffee, then said, "Trust me, I was skeptical, too. So I started asking some questions in Blowing Rock, flashing Earnest's picture around to see if I could get any nibbles. It took some doing, but I found a woman who knew him, and had even been to his house once for a party. I checked it out, and the mailbox said Bliss. That's a common enough synonym for Joy, wouldn't you say? The place was spectacular, Ben. When I checked the county records, the house and land were registered to a corporation called Delight Industries. He wasn't too careful about hiding his connections, was he?"

I rubbed my chin. "So where does that leave us?"

"I'm not sure," my grandfather said. "When I got back

home from Blowing Rock, somebody left a message on my doorstep. I'm not afraid to admit that it kind of shook me. That's when I asked you to meet me at The Hound Dog."

"What was it?" I asked. I knew my grandfather wasn't that easy to intimidate.

"There was a dagger sticking into a bar of our soap. Whoever left the message for me knew how to get to me. Ben, I took it as a threat against our entire family. Whoever did it heated the blade hot enough to embed it into the bar. I'm not afraid to say that it rattled me pretty good."

"So that's why you've been in hiding. Did you tell Molly all of this?"

He nodded. "I did, just before I left. She said she'd look into it."

"Blast it all, she should have told me," I said, the anger flowing through me.

Paulus put a hand on mine. "I asked her not to, Ben. It was my decision, not hers. If you're going to be angry with anybody, it should be with me."

That took some of the anger out of me. "I know you had your reasons, but you should have told me."

"I'm an old man," he said. "Maybe I made a mistake erring on the side of caution."

I'd never seen him so humble. "It's fine. You're not keeping anything else from me, are you?"

He shook his head. "That's it. Evidently I attracted some unwanted attention when I was snooping around. I'm afraid I bungled it."

"You did fine," I said, "and you dug up more than I managed to get."

"So what are you going to do now?"

I looked steadily at him and said, "I'm going to keep looking."

"Ben, it's dangerous. Think of the family."

I snapped, "I am. The best way to protect them is to solve this case and end the threat. Otherwise, we're all going to be looking over our shoulders for the rest of our lives."

He appeared to think about that, then said, "You're right. Funny, I would have probably felt the exact same way myself thirty years ago. What should we do next?"

"I think you did exactly the right thing, Paulus," I said. "Whoever you spooked is looking for you. Can you stay in Sassafras Ridge until I get this mess straightened out? How are you set for money?"

"I'm fine," he said. "As a matter of fact, I'm sleeping on Lois's couch."

I remembered the crabby woman I'd talked to a few days before. "Listen, I can float you a loan if you want to get a hotel room instead."

"I wouldn't go back to the Beverly Inn if they were giving rooms away, and the other place I was staying was a real dump. Besides, Lois isn't as bad as she must seem to you. She's good company when she wants to be."

"If you're sure," I said.

Paulus studied me a few moments, then asked, "What are you going to do now, Ben?"

"I'm going to try to find out how Earnest Joy managed to accumulate so much money under everyone else's radar." I handed him my cell phone. "Keep this. I might have to call you if I need something else."

"I hate those things," he said, staring at my phone as if it were a snake.

"Yeah, well, I don't want to lose you again." I took a bite of pie.

"If I keep in touch, will you take it with you? I don't want it."

I picked my phone up and stuck it in my pocket. "Fine. But I expect you to call Kate at the shop every day. Understood?"

"If it will keep me from using one of those things, I'd agree to just about anything."

I grabbed his check as well as mine as I stood. "I'll take care of this on the way out."

"I can buy my own meals," he said, reaching for the bill.

"You get the tip and we'll call it even," I said.

He reluctantly agreed, and we walked out of the Lazy Spoon together. Paulus patted me on the back. "Good luck, Ben, and be careful."

"You know it," I said. As I drove back to Harper's Landing, I tried to figure out how Earnest had accumulated enough money to live the extravagant lifestyle he was enjoying at the resort community. I wondered if his own children even knew about his second home. Or other name. Andrew wouldn't tell me even if the truth would suit his purposes better, but I still had a relationship with Terri, no matter how tenuous it was at the time.

When I got back to Harper's Landing, I drove to the jewelry store instead of the soap shop. If I was lucky, Terri would be working. But if Andrew was there instead, I was still going to grill him. And if he happened to take a swing at me when things got rough, I wouldn't pass up an opportunity to put him on the floor. The animosity between us hadn't eased over the years, and though I was a bit surprised myself by how much I disliked him, I couldn't do anything to soften it. Andrew knew the exact spot to push to get me going, and my reactions were beyond my understanding. I'd have to watch my temper and keep it in check, though. Protecting my family took priority, and I had to stay focused on that.

When I walked in the door of the jewelry shop, I saw Terri standing alone behind the counter. Some of the tension went out of me, and I realized I'd been bracing myself for a confrontation with her brother.

Terri wasn't all that happy to see me. "Ben, you might as well drop your pretense about buying something for your new girlfriend. I know what you're doing."

I nodded. "I am dating someone new, but you're right. I'm trying to find out who killed your father. I would think you and your brother would want to help me, not block me every time you could."

"We think you should leave it up to the police," she said. "Of course we both want Dad's killer caught."

"Let me ask you one thing, then I'll get out of your hair. How do you like Blowing Rock?"

"What's that got to do with anything?" she asked.

"I'm just curious," I said.

"I think it's overpriced. Whenever I go through there on my sales route, I eat in Lenoir before I go up 321. Why?"

"So you don't ever stay there?" I pushed.

"It's two hours from here," she said. "I won't stay anywhere that close to home overnight if I can help it."

"How about your father? Has he spent much time there lately?"

She had clearly had enough of my questioning, but she replied, "He mentioned a few times that he enjoyed the mountains, but that's about it. Ben, what has this got to do with anything?"

If she was lying to me, she was very good at it. "What

would you say if I told you your father had a second home up there, a nicer place than the one he lived in here?"

"I'd say you've lost your mind. If you'd ever seen our books, you'd know what a ridiculous idea that is."

"Still, it looks like it's true. So if he didn't make the money through this shop, where did it come from? Did he have any other sources of income?"

She shook her head. "Not that I know of, but I wasn't privy to all of his businesses. I knew he liked to dabble in things on the side, but there's no way he could make the kind of money you're talking about without me knowing about it."

"How about Andrew?" I asked. "Would he know?"

Terri laughed. "He was even less in the loop than I was. Ralph Haller probably knew more than either one of us did. They even had a business together."

"Do you know what they were doing?" I asked. This could be the break I'd been hoping for.

"No, you'll have to ask Ralph. I've never been a big fan of the man, and he's never cared for me either, truth be told. There's something that's shifty about him, you know?"

"Trust me, I agree with you. You know he's been in jail, don't you?"

"Twice," she said. "Dad said he was reformed, though, and he wouldn't listen to a bad word about Ralph."

That was news to me. "I knew he'd gone to prison for burglary," I said, "but what else was he convicted of?"

"I don't have a clue," she said. "Ben, don't ask me anything else. If Andrew knew I was talking to you now he'd have a stroke. I don't know why you two have always hated each other, but it's pretty obvious to the world that you do. I'd appreciate it if you'd just let this drop."

"I can't, not with my name on top of the police's list of suspects."

She shrugged. "I suppose I understand that, but don't ask for my help anymore, okay? I'm trying to put this all behind me, and every time you come in, I have nightmares all over again."

"I'm truly sorry about that," I said as I left.

I thought about going over to Ralph's house to ask him about his second conviction, but I sincerely doubted he'd tell me the truth. When I'd been at the library looking into his history, I'd stopped the second I'd found a reference to him. It looked like I needed to do a little more research.

Corki was still behind the reference desk, scanning a book about ancient Egypt. The second she saw me, she closed the book. "Please tell me you've brought me something challenging today."

"As a matter of fact, I think I might have missed something the last time I was here."

She smiled. "I thought you might be back. I would have called you, but I didn't know your name."

I extended a hand. "I'm Ben Perkins."

She pointed to her nametag. "And you already know I'm Corki. Hang on one second, I made a copy of it and filed it away." She browsed through an accordion file filled with papers. As she looked, Corki explained, "When I get an intriguing question, I keep digging sometimes. It's a lot of fun." She studied a sheet, then pulled it out. "Here it is. We finally got the printer working. Is this what you're looking for?"

I studied the reproduction of the newspaper article and saw that Terri had been right about Ralph. There was another conviction I'd missed the last time. The brief article said that two years after being released from his burglary sentence, Haller had been tried and convicted for counter-feiting. I remembered that Molly had complained that she'd been working on a counterfeiting case in Harper's Landing, as well as Earnest Joy's murder. Could the two be connected? I started playing with scenarios until I came up with something that fit. If Ralph and Earnest were working together on something illegal and highly profitable, it could be reason enough for murder. Ralph could make the bad bills and Earnest could distribute them on his travels searching for artifacts to convert into jewelry. It could be a profitable sideline for both of them, unless Ralph got too greedy and wanted a bigger stake.

I thanked her, then started for the door.

Corki said, "You look like you're in a hurry to get somewhere."

"I am," I said as I raced off to find Molly. This was the kind of proof I needed. If only she'd believe me.

IT took me half an hour to track her down, but I finally found Molly at the courthouse.

"I need to talk to you," I said.

"Sorry, I don't have much time. I'm waiting to testify in a case."

"This is important," I said.

Molly stared at me a few seconds, then reluctantly said, "Go ahead."

"I think I've got it all figured out."

"What's that, all of the problems in your life? Congrat-ulations."

"I'm talking about Earnest Joy's murder."

She looked around us, then hissed, "Keep your voice down, Ben. The last thing I need is for everyone in town to know that you're digging into this."

In a softer voice, I said, "You never told me Ralph went to prison twice. I just found out that the second time, he was convicted of counterfeiting. Didn't you tell me you were working on a case that involved counterfeiting? What if Ralph and Earnest were partners, and Ralph got greedy?"

She actually laughed loud enough for the people nearby to look at us.

"What's so funny?" I asked.

"This is exactly why I don't like amateurs trying to get involved in my cases. There are a few things wrong with your theory. Would you like to hear them, or should I trot over to Ralph's house and arrest him on your say-so?"

"I'm listening," I said.

She replied, "Here goes. Ralph was convicted of passing bad twenties, and the counterfeit case I'm working on isn't money at all. At least nothing you could spend in a convenience store. Second, I already looked into that possibility, and Ralph was in the dentist's office waiting for his appointment. Doc Lace was running behind, and he sat there for three hours waiting to be seen when Joy was murdered. So much for your theory. By the way, thanks for the bum steer earlier."

"What are you talking about?"

She looked upset. "I drove out to the Mountain Lake Motel to talk to this Linda Mae, but she wasn't there."

"So go back later. I'm sure she was probably just shopping or something."

Molly shook her head. "You don't understand. When I say she wasn't there, that's exactly what I meant. She checked out, and on her way she told the desk clerk she was getting as far away from Harper's Landing as fast as she could. He said something had spooked her, and she tore out of the parking lot like she was on fire."

"You need to talk to her, Molly. She might have had something to do with this."

Molly snorted. "So now you're shifting the blame to Linda Mae? Wow, that was quick, even for you. Go home, Ben."

I wasn't giving up that easily, though. There was something else I wanted to know. "What kind of counterfeiting case are you working on if it's not money?"

She started to answer when a bailiff came out of the courtroom. "Molly, they're ready for you now."

"Sorry, Ben. I've got to go. Why don't you give it a rest? I've got it covered."

After she slipped into the courtroom, I decided to go talk to Kelly. If Linda Mae had really left town, her attorney would know it. I was dreading the conversation with Kelly, but I couldn't help it. I walked across the street and into her office.

Her receptionist was there, talking on the phone as he filed some papers in his drawer.

"Yes, Ma'am. Hold on one second." He cradled the telephone between his cheek and his shoulder and asked, "May I help you?"

"I need to see Kelly."

He rolled his eyes. "Haven't we gone over this before? Without an appointment, you can't get in. Sorry." He didn't seem to be sorry at all.

We were both surprised when Kelly walked out of her office. "Ben? I thought I heard your voice. Come on back."

The receptionist looked at me as if he wanted to set fire

to me. It was all I could do not to smile at him as I walked past him into the inner sanctum.

There were a thousand things I wanted to say to Kelly, and none of them had to do with Earnest Joy's murder. She looked absolutely lovely in her business suit with her blonde hair pulled back, though I still preferred her in blue jeans.

"Ben, I'm not sure why you're here," she said.

"I need to ask you something. Is Linda Mae still in town?" I asked.

"What? Is that why you came here?" She looked startled by my question, as if she'd expected something completely different.

"I saw her going into your office yesterday, and I need to know if you're her attorney."

"I can't tell you that," she said.

"Don't give me some guff about attorney–client privilege," I said. "This is important."

"And my principles aren't?" Kelly asked.

"Is she gone?" I asked.

Kelly looked as if she wanted to cry. It was hard seeing the saddened expression on her face. She was normally a strong, vibrant woman. Had my presence done this to her? No, there had to be something else going on in her life.

She sighed, then admitted, "I don't know why I'm sparring with you. She's not a client."

"I saw her here," I said.

"She came by," Kelly admitted. "But after we talked, she decided to drop her case. The woman has absolutely no proof that she and Earnest Joy were ever married. All it took was one call to the Bureau of Records in Clark County to prove that." Kelly's voice softened as she added, "How are you, Ben?"

"I've been better," I said. "How about you?"

She shrugged as her receptionist came in, handing her a briefcase.

"Sorry to interrupt," he said, "but you're late."

She glanced at the clock, then said, "Ben, I've got to go. Sorry to make this so short."

"I got what I came for," I said. "Thanks for the information."

We walked out of the office together, but didn't share another word until she said good-bye in a muted voice. It had been pretty painful for me to be around her, but she'd dumped me. So why was she acting that way? Maybe it was guilt from the way she'd handled it. I couldn't be mad at her anymore, though. Kelly was trying to put her family back together, and I knew it couldn't be easy for her. The best thing I could do was to stay away from her.

I drove toward the soap shop, but I couldn't take the grilling I was going to get from the family, at least not yet. I decided to circle the block a few times to clear my head. As I approached the jewelry store—a natural part of my route—I looked toward the front door and saw a woman coming out. She looked familiar, but with a scarf covering most of her face and large, dark sunglasses over her eyes, it was hard to say who she was. Then I saw her beige raincoat open and underneath it, I caught a glimpse of leopard capri pants. It had to be Linda Mae! But she was supposed to be out of town, according to Molly. I tried to find a place to pull over, but by the time I'd realized it was her, I was past the store, and there was no place else to park on the street. When I finally managed to find a spot to pull the Miata into, I raced back to the shop on foot, but she was gone. I hesitated before going into the jewelry store. If there was another body in there waiting to be found, I didn't want to be the one to stumble over it. I peeked in through the front window, and saw Terri working on one of the displays with jewelry made from gold coins.

At least she was safe. As quietly as I could, I slipped away and walked back to my car.

I was nearly there when I heard an ambulance racing down the street. My stomach did a flip as it neared. I had a feeling that I knew exactly where it was going.

AS I suspected, it was headed toward the nearby neighborhood where Earnest Joy and Ralph Haller lived. I'd pictured Ralph as the killer, but what if there had been a third partner in the operation? Could he have taken drastic action to get the whole pie? It sounded far-fetched even to me, and I wouldn't dare try it out on Molly. Okay, forgetting the phantom third partner for a second, maybe someone knew what Ralph and Earnest were up to. Could they have tried to move in on the scam, whatever it was that had afforded Earnest Joy's expensive getaway? Possibilities were flying through my mind as I neared their street. I was surprised to see the ambulance in front of the Joy house, not the Haller place, though. As I got there, they were wheeling someone out on a gurney.

ELEVEN

o o o

I pulled up just as Molly got on the scene. She shook her head when she saw me. "You're making a habit of this, aren't you?"

"I thought you were in court," I said.

"After he saw me waiting to testify, Frank Jordan decided to take the plea bargain he'd been offered before. It was a smart move. I was getting ready to nail him."

Molly approached one of the attendants as they loaded the stretcher into the back of the ambulance. "What happened?"

"It looks like a suicide attempt," he said as he worked to secure the gurney in the vehicle.

I looked in and saw Andrew Joy's face partially obscured by an oxygen mask.

Molly asked, "What did he try to do? There's no blood."

"This one went with pills. There are enough empty bottles in there to stock a pharmacy. We've got to roll."

After they sped away, Molly turned to me. Before she

could say anything, I said, "Hey, I had nothing to do with this, either."

"I know that," she said. "You don't have any business being here, though."

"Can I come in with you, anyway?" I asked. "It's not like it's a crime scene or anything."

Molly shook her head. "I'm not willing to say that until I've had a look around. Go home, Ben."

"I think I'll stick around," I said. "I want to see what you find out."

"What makes you think I'll tell you anything, even if I do find something out?"

"I can hope, can't I?"

She didn't say anything as she headed into the house. I waited outside, half expecting Ralph Haller to come out and accuse me of attempted murder.

Where was Ralph? The ambulance's sirens and flashing lights should have brought him out like a shot. If he was home.

I decided to walk over there and nose around. Maybe he'd left something in plain sight that he shouldn't have.

I walked to the front door, rang it twice, then pounded on the frame. "Ralph. It's Ben Perkins. I need to talk to you."

Nothing. I peered in through the side window, but though the curtain was still askew, I couldn't see anything out of the ordinary. The place was still a mess, and it made looking for clues even harder. I decided to get a better view, so I walked around to the side of the house and tried to look in one of the windows. From next door, I heard Molly shout from the porch, "Get away from there. Do I have to arrest you for trespassing to keep you out of trouble?"

"I'm just looking for Ralph," I said.

"Well stop peeping in through his windows, will you?"

She walked back into the house, and I started toward my car when Ralph's trash can caught my eye. He'd already wheeled it to the curb, and I found myself wondering if he'd thrown anything incriminating away. I flipped the lid off the can and grabbed the top bag. If he'd done anything lately, it would be in that bag. At least it didn't reek. I drove off before Molly could arrest me for stealing garbage and headed back to the soap shop. I would have liked the privacy of my apartment to sort through Ralph's trash—especially if it turned out to be a dead end—but there was no way I was going to spread his refuse out on my coffee table.

I parked on the fresh asphalt in back and took a cardboard box out of the recycling bin. Cindy was a nut for saving the environment every chance she could, and I'd found that she'd actually started to convert me to her side. I cut the cardboard until I had a large, flat surface and tore the bag open.

At first glance, there was nothing there worth seeing. I took a stick and sorted through take-out bags from every fast-food joint in town, and I wondered if the man ever ate a meal he'd prepared himself. I was one of the world's worst cooks, but I still managed to feed myself better than that. The problem was that all of the takeout refuse obscured the rest of the trash. I ducked inside the shop, grabbed a pair of work gloves and a trash bag, then started back outside.

Jeff was there working by himself, and I thought he was going to ignore me completely when he asked, "Cleaning up the landscaping, Ben?"

"Something like that," I said, without explaining myself any further. I wasn't quite ready to apologize for my earlier behavior yet.

Back outside, I started tossing the wrappings from Ralph's meals in the fresh bag, and by the time I'd gotten rid of everything in that category, I had nearly cleaned off the cardboard. There were a few wadded up paper towels that I almost chucked as well when I saw that one of them was coated with some kind of grayish black material. After pulling that aside, I went through the rest of the trash, but didn't find anything else.

As I chucked the trash bag into the Dumpster, Jeff finally came out. "Okay, I give up. What are you up to?"

Instead of answering his question directly, I handed him the paper towel. "Does that look familiar to you?"

Jeff grabbed it, studied the stains for a second, then held it up to his nose. "It's got some kind of chemical base," he said, "but I can't say more than that. You know who you should ask?" I'd expected him to say Bob, but he said, "Jim would probably know what it is."

"Not Bob?"

"He might know," Jeff admitted, "but he's in Charlotte trying to find a new main burner. The old one's just about shot." We melted a great deal of soap aggregate on our production line, and I knew the burner was crucial to our operation.

"So where's Jim?" I asked.

"He's in Charlotte with Bob," Jeff said, trying to hide a growing smile.

"You nit," I said, happy for a taste of the old relationship I'd had with my brother before he'd started dating Molly.

"Listen, we need to talk," I said.

"Do we have to?"

"I do if I'm going to apologize. I don't know what's gotten into me lately, but I'm sorry for the way I've been behaving, okay?"

He looked at me as if he was waiting for the punch line.

"I'm serious," I said. "You should be able to date whoever you want without worrying about me. Do you forgive me?"

"There's nothing to forgive," he said. "I understand where you're coming from."

I nodded, then said, "Now, are you ready to apologize to me?"

He looked at me cryptically, so I explained. "You've been walking around here like the head rooster in the hen-house. Maybe you should take it down a notch or two, okay?"

"Has it been that obvious?" he asked.

"Not unless you're blind," I answered.

"Sorry about that," he said.

I put an arm around his neck, gave it an affectionate hug, then released him and said, "You're forgiven."

I started inside, and he followed me. Grabbing a plastic baggie, I stuffed the paper towel into it and sealed it. I wasn't sure what it meant, but I wanted to ask one of my other brothers before I threw it away. I hadn't been wrong about digging through Ralph's trash. Maybe I'd just got the wrong bag.

I headed back out the rear exit when Jeff asked, "Where are you going?"

"Trash can diving," I said. "Want to come along?"

"No, thanks."

This time I was going to get every bag out of his can, but just as I got there, the garbage truck was pulling away from Ralph's house. I'd just missed them.

I was going to give up when I heard Molly hail me from the front porch of the Joy house. "Are you still here?"

Instead of telling her about my trash scavenging, I said, "Did you honestly think I'd give up that easily?"

She looked around, saw that no one was watching us, then said, "You might as well come on in. I know you'll never stop bugging me until I let you see what's inside."

I raced up the sidewalk toward her. Before she'd let me inside, she said, "First things first. You are not to touch anything, do you understand? If I catch you so much as breathing on something in this house, I'm going to lock you up for the fun of it. Are we clear?"

"Yes, ma'am," I said.

"Come on in, then."

I followed her into the house, but we didn't have to go far once we were inside. There were seven or eight empty pill bottles sitting on the coffee table in the living room, and a nearly empty quart of whiskey beside them.

"He wasn't taking any chances, was he?" I asked in a hushed tone. "Was there a note?"

"They don't always leave notes, Ben," she said.

"Hey, take it easy. I was just asking."

Molly shook her head. "No, no note. So what do you think happened?"

I studied the scene, then said, "My guess is he killed his dad, then couldn't live with the guilt. But I don't get it. You know Andrew. Can you honestly imagine him passing up the opportunity to get the last word in?"

Molly looked down at the tableau again. "You've got a point. I'll be interested to hear what he says about it. You know, he might deny it was a suicide attempt at all if they manage to revive him. I've heard half a dozen people who were clearly trying to kill themselves come up with the most bizarre explanations of how it was all just an accident."

"So what do we do in the meantime? Are you going to have everything dusted for fingerprints?"

"This isn't a television program, Ben," she said.

"There's no doubt in my mind this is exactly what it looks like."

"Well, there's doubt in mine. At least collect the bottles and have them checked. That's not too tough to do, is it?"

"Will it get you off my back?" she asked.

"It's a start," I admitted. Molly pulled a few bags out of her kit and collected the bottles. "Don't forget the whiskey," I said.

She didn't say a word, but the look she shot me was more than enough to convey her thoughts.

"Now what?" I asked her.

"I take this to the lab and have them dust for prints. Then we wait to see if Andrew comes out of it. Come on, let's go."

"You go ahead," I said. "I want to look around a little more."

She grabbed my arm and walked me out of the house.

"Hey, it was worth a shot," I said.

"Do you really think so?"

I stopped on the front steps. "Molly, how did you hear about this?"

"The dispatcher called me and told me an ambulance was on its way. Why?"

I scratched my chin. "I'm just wondering. Who called them? If Andrew was trying to kill himself, why did he dial 911? If someone else was in on it, why screw it up? Did they get cold feet?"

She frowned at me, and I knew that despite her expression, I'd made a point worth considering.

"Hang on a second." She walked to her squad car, picked up the mike, and had a brief conversation.

As she rejoined me, she said, "It turns out that he called it in himself. From the sound of it, Andrew had second thoughts."

"So it was a dead end," I said.

"No, I should have asked the same question myself. You're not as dim as you usually seem, Ben."

"I'm all aglow with your kind words," I said as I got into my Miata and watched her drive off. Frankly, I didn't know what else to do. Until Andrew came out of it, if he ever did, we wouldn't know what had forced him to such drastic measures. What would be a better reason to commit suicide, though, than if he'd killed his own father? Sometimes the simplest answer is the right one.

I would have loved to talk to Ralph, but his car was still missing from his driveway, and I had no idea when he might come home. Did I really want to be the one who told him that Andrew had tried to kill himself? There was little doubt in my mind that when he heard about what had happened, the man would somehow try to blame me for it.

It was getting late, so I decided to swing by Diana's bookstore to see if I could cash that rain check for dinner I'd taken earlier.

She was just locking up as I parked in front of the store. "That's some bad timing, isn't it?" I asked as she turned and saw me approach.

"I don't mind opening back up for you," she said. "Are you looking for something to read?"

"Actually, I was hoping your offer to go to The Hound Dog was still open."

"Sorry, I've already eaten," she said, "but there's always room for dessert. How about some pie? My treat."

"That's hardly a fair exchange for the dinner I provided," I said, smiling at her. "You can do better than that, can't you?"

She pretended to think about it, then said, "I'll throw in a scoop of ice cream, but that's my best offer."

I held the passenger door of the Miata open for her. "Now you're talking."

We found a booth near a window at The Hound Dog, and I helped Diana take her jacket off.

Ruby approached us, and I said, "Let's clear a few things up first. I'm here on a date with this young lady, and she's paying."

Ruby studied Diana for a second, then said, "How did he trick you into that?"

"He took me to The Lakeside Inn for dinner," Diana said.

"That sounds like a fair trade to me," Ruby said. She pointed her pencil at me and held her pad up. "What will you have?"

"I'll take a slice of cherry pie, and top it with some vanilla ice cream."

Diana replied, "That sounds good to me. Make it two."

Ruby said, "Coming right up. Any requests for the juke box?"

I said, "What do you think, Diana?"

She slid a quarter across the table. "How about your café's namesake?"

Ruby winked at her. "That's my girl. Excellent choice."

A minute later Elvis was singing about hound dogs. I said, "I hope that's not directed at me."

Diana laughed, a sound I was growing to love. "I figured it was Ruby's favorite. Why else name her business after it?"

We chatted about a few little things as we waited for our pie, but Andrew's name didn't come up. The last thing I wanted to talk about was his botched suicide attempt. I wanted to get away from all of that and enjoy my time with Diana.

Ruby brought our plates, the slices properly topped with ice cream.

Diana's spoon poised over the top. "I really shouldn't."

"Why on earth not?" I asked as I took a bite.

"I'm constantly counting calories," she admitted.

"I don't see why. I think you look great. As a matter of fact, you could use an extra pound or two."

She smiled. "Thank you, but you're lying. Still, that's all the encouragement I need." She took a bite, then said, "That's incredible."

"Garnet makes her own crust in back," I said. "She and Ruby are quite a team."

After we finished our desserts, I reached for the check, out of habit more than anything else.

Diana snatched it away before I could get it. "Hey, I'm picking that up, remember?"

"I'm just hoping if I buy tonight, you'll invite me out someplace else tomorrow night."

She frowned. "I would if I could, but Rufus actually has a date himself, if you can believe that. I'm watching the store by myself. Can we do it another night?"

"Absolutely," I said.

I drove Diana back to her shop. "You don't have to get out," she said. "I'm parked over there."

I popped out of my door. "Hang on a second." As I opened her door, I asked, "I'm sorry, now what did you say?"

She grinned. "You heard me. How gallant of you to walk me to my car."

I followed her, then asked, "How else am I going to get a good-night kiss? This did qualify as a date, didn't it?"

She turned into my arms and kissed me as her answer. After a few seconds, she said, "What do you think?"

"I think pie's my new favorite dessert," I said.

She giggled and opened her door. "Thanks for tonight. That was fun."

"It was indeed." After she drove off, I saw a car start up and drive away right after she did. It had been sitting there the entire time I'd been with Diana, but I hadn't noticed it until it was gone.

It was Kelly's car. Either by accident or design, she'd seen me kiss Diana good night. I felt a pang about it, but there wasn't anything I could do, so I drove home. Before going to bed, I called the hospital to check on Andrew's condition. They wouldn't tell me anything, so I asked if Terri was there. She was, and soon picked up the telephone.

"How's he doing?" I asked her.

"I'm surprised you care," she said. "When did you suddenly get so concerned about my brother's well being?"

"I saw the ambulance, and I watched them take him to the hospital," I said. "I don't want to see him dead, Terri, despite what you may think."

She softened slightly. "Sorry, I overreacted. They're not sure yet. He's in a drug-induced coma, and the doctor just told me right now all we can do is wait and see."

"I hope he pulls through," I said. It was true there was no love lost between Andrew and me, but I was hoping if he came to, he'd confess so that we could all put the murder behind us.

"That's sweet of you," she said.

"By the way, I saw your stepmother leaving the jewelry store this afternoon. I thought she left town for good."

"What are you talking about? She never came by, not when I was working."

"Terri, I saw her. I admit the disguise was a decent one, but no one else in Harper's Landing wears capri pants like those."

"I don't know what you're talking about, Ben. Thanks for calling," she said, then hung up.

That was odd. Why would she deny Linda Mae's visit, when I'd seen her myself? Could she be hiding something? I wondered if Linda Mae was pursuing another angle, since she'd given up on the legal one. Could she know something about Earnest Joy that would be worthy of blackmail, even after the man's death?

I had more questions than answers, and I knew it would be a fitful night's sleep. At least maybe my slumbering thoughts could lead me to the truth, since I wasn't doing all that well awake.

THE next morning, all I had resolved through the night was that I needed a new mattress. I tried calling the hospital to see if Andrew Joy's condition had changed overnight, but they wouldn't tell me over the telephone. When I asked for Terri, I was told curtly that she hadn't left her brother's side all night, and that she was refusing all calls. I couldn't fault her for that. Family came first with my clan. There was no reason in the world to think that it wouldn't be their top priority, too.

I went to the soap shop, figuring that while I was waiting for news, I might as well get some work done. It was twenty minutes before we were due to open when I got there, and my three sisters were working at stocking the shelves and straightening things as they went along.

"Good morning, ladies," I said.

"Hey, Ben."

"Hello."

"Yo," Cindy said.

I raised an eyebrow as I looked at her. "Yo?"

"I just wanted to be different," she said with a smile.

"Okay," I said. "Do any of you have connections at the

hospital? I'm trying to find out Andrew Joy's condition, and they're stonewalling me."

Louisa said, "Jenny Bartlett works there. Give me a second."

Before she dialed, I said, "I don't want you to put a strain on your friendship."

Louisa laughed. "Please. She owes me big time." She turned to Kate and said, "Remember when Paul Jones got married, and Jenny wanted to crash the wedding because she thought she was his one true love? Man, she was drunk that night."

Kate shook her head. "I couldn't believe it when you told her you'd drive her to the wedding yourself. I thought you'd lost your mind."

"I had to get her into the car, didn't I? After she threw up, I was wishing I'd driven hers. I'd say she can do this for me."

I clapped my hands. "Ladies, can we focus here?"

Louisa stuck her tongue out at me. "Let me ask."

She carried on a whispered conversation, then put her hand over the phone. "This will just take a second."

"Thanks, Louisa, I appreciate you doing this."

"I'm happy to do it. I've been meaning to call Jenny anyway. What?" she said into the receiver. "Okay, thanks. Yeah, lunch tomorrow sounds good. Just no Bloody Marys, okay?" Louisa laughed, then hung up.

"There's no change, but she'll call as soon as there is."

"You know what?" I said. "Sometimes it's good having such a big family."

Cindy said, "Sometimes? What does that mean, brother dear?"

"I'll leave it to your imagination." I looked at her, then I said, "I thought you were off this morning." Mom had asked me to help cover the floor, and I'd agreed, since I didn't have any other ideas to pursue at the moment.

"I've got a dentist appointment," she admitted. "But it's not for another ten minutes."

"Shoo," I said. "We can struggle through the morning without you."

Cindy shrugged. "I guess." She grabbed her coat and left.

I started for the back when Kate said, "Hey, I thought you were going to work with us this morning since we're going to be one short."

"I am," I said. "I just need to ask Bob and Jim something."

Kate tapped her watch. "Just as long as you're back here when we open."

I saluted. "Yes, ma'am."

I took the baggie with the paper towel from my pocket as I walked back to the line. Bob had his head under the old burner while Jim stood nearby handing him tools. Jeff was offering his own commentary as I approached.

"Now I know why there were only three stooges," I said. "That's plenty enough for trouble."

From under the boiler, I heard Bob say, "Don't forget Shep. That makes four in my book."

Jim said, "Not four at the same time, though. It was always three."

"I could swear all four of them were on one show," Jeff said.

Jim threw a rag at him. "Yeah, you also claim you've seen a UFO, remember?"

"Hey, it didn't look like a weather balloon to me. I don't care what the newspaper said."

"Guys, I need to ask you something," I said.

Bob said, "Fire away." He paused, then asked, "What's

wrong with you guys? That was funny. I'm working on the boiler, and I said fire away."

Jeff said, "Oh, it was funny. You just can't see my reaction, because I'm laughing on the inside."

Jim asked, "What was it you wanted to know? You don't need these two clowns, I can answer any question you need answered."

"Unless it's about your love life; he's a wash there," Bob said.

"Or anything factual in any way," Jeff chimed in. "Other than that, he's your man."

I handed the baggie to Jim. "What is it?"

He took the paper towel out of the baggie, studied it a moment, then lifted it to his nose. "Beats me."

"So much for an expert opinion," Jeff said.

"Then you tell him what it is," Jim snapped.

I said, "He already tried."

"And failed," Jeff answered with a smile.

"Bob, I hate to ask," I said, "but do you have a second?"

"Sure, I was planning to take a break anyway." He crawled out from under the boiler where the old burner was still firmly in place.

"Having some trouble with that?" I asked.

"No, I enjoy lying on the concrete on my back scraping my knuckles. I can't put the new one on if I can't get the old one off, you know what I mean?"

I looked at the replacement burner, and was amazed how good it looked. "Where in the world did you find that?"

Bob said, "It's not that hard, if you just know where to look."

Jim slapped Bob's shoulder. "Don't let him lie to you.

We scavenged through junkyards all day yesterday until he found that. It was buried under a coat of grease so thick I couldn't even tell what it was. I kept telling him all the way home last night that it would never work, so the fool stayed up all night getting it in shape."

Bob stifled a yawn. "It was worth it. What's the mystery, Ben?"

Jim handed him the paper towel, and I watched Bob go through the same process Jim had done. He frowned a second, then smiled. "I know what it is."

"Don't keep us in suspense," I said. "What is it?"

"It's a chemical used to antique things. I've seen it before. It takes shiny metal and makes it black. Really, it's kind of cool."

That didn't make sense. "Are you sure it's not some kind of cleaner?" I'd been so sure that Ralph had been cleaning those coins, but could he have been doing just the opposite?

"I'm sure. It's a different smell altogether," he said. "Now if you ladies will excuse me, I seem to be the only one working here today."

"Hey, that's not fair," Jim said. "I'm handing you tools."

"And I'm giving you some much-needed advice," Jeff protested.

"I'm working the front," I said.

Bob held his grease-stained hands up. "I apologize, on all counts. You are all working harder than I am." He shook his head, but I could see the smile he was trying to hide as he slid back under the boiler.

I went up front to tell my sisters I had an errand to run when I saw that we were already open for business. Kate was running the floor today since it was one of Mom's rare days off, so I decided to tell her and escape before Louisa could protest.

"Ben, you're just the person we're looking for."

That's when I noticed Herbert and Constance standing with her. Constance had a Tupperware bowl in her hands as Herbert said, "That's not entirely true. We were looking for Cindy, but she's not here, so I guess you'll have to do."

"Herbert, be civil," Constance said. There was no doubt in my mind that if she hadn't been holding the bowl in both hands, she would have elbowed her spouse. I saw Kate move away from the conversation, and wished I could join her.

"What can I do for you?" I asked, hoping to make it quick so I could get back to my investigation.

"Tell us how to fix this," Constance said as she took the lid off her bowl. Inside it was a concoction that looked like cottage cheese gone bad, with lumps of soap floating in a viscous liquid.

Herbert volunteered, "We were hand-milling last night and this is what we got. The stuff wouldn't set up, even overnight."

"Let me guess," I said as I studied the mess. "You used a lot of additives when you combined it."

Constance said, "Maybe I went a little overboard, but I've done it with pours before and it was fine."

"Hand-milling is different," I said. "Your soap is curdled, but I can fix this. Maybe."

Herbert sneered down at the bowl. "I don't see how."

"Let's go back to the classroom," I said, taking the bowl from Constance's hands.

I measured out some fresh soap noodles, added water, and set the pot on the hot plate. In no time at all I had nice melt, so I added the contents of Constance's bowl into the pot and let that combine. I poured the new melt into one of our molds and handed it to them.

"Give this six to twelve hours, then see what you've got. I'm not giving you any guarantees, but it might do the trick."

"What if it doesn't?" Herbert asked.

"Then toss it out and start over," I said.

Constance said, "I'm sure it will work. Thank you, Ben."

Herbert nodded. "Yeah, you're almost as good as your sister."

"Herbert," his wife snapped.

"Honestly, I'm glad to hear you like Cindy's teaching," I said.

"She's very good, but so are you," Constance said.

Herbert said, "Quit trying to butter him up. He's not your teacher anymore."

"I'm just being polite, and you know it."

Her husband added, "Don't try to convince me, woman. You're the one who's protesting too much."

After they were gone, Kate drifted back toward me. "What was that all about?"

"They had a problem with a hand-mill," I said.

Kate looked at me a second, then said, "I hope you're not upset that they asked for Cindy first."

"Are you kidding me? I'm elated. I've always thought she'd make a wonderful teacher. I'm just thrilled I've been proven right."

Kate kissed my cheek. "You want to know something? You're the best big brother any of us could ask for."

"Thanks," I said.

Louisa was on the phone, and she looked shaken when she hung up. "Ben, that was the hospital."

"What happened? Is there any news about Andrew?"

She nodded. "He just died."

TWELVE

○ ○ ○

"**WHERE** are you going?" Kate asked me as I bolted for the door.

"I need to talk to Terri." I had to know if Andrew had come out of it before he'd died. If he'd confessed to the murder, it would take the heat off me entirely.

"Don't push her too hard," Louisa said. "She just lost a brother and a father in less than a week. She's going to be a basket case."

"I'll be gentle," I said.

I drove ten miles over the speed limit as I raced to the hospital. I had to talk to Terri. To my surprise, I found her in the parking lot wandering aimlessly around.

I pulled into a spot, then said, "Terri, are you all right?"

"I can't find my car," she said, her voice near hysteria. "It was here, I know it, and now it's gone. Help me find it, Ben."

"Tell you what, why don't you get in the Miata and I'll drive you around until we come across it." I didn't want her driving in that condition, but short of forcing her into my car, I didn't know how else to accomplish that.

Thankfully, she let me help her into the Miata.

Once we were moving, I said, "I'm so sorry about Andrew."

"I'm in shock," she said. "Last week I had a family, and suddenly I'm all alone." There were tears running down her cheeks, though her voice was firm.

"Did he ever wake up?" I asked.

"Why do you ask?" she said.

"I'm just wondering if he said anything about your father. Terri, I've got the sneaking suspicion that Andrew might have had something to do with what happened to him." It was a real risk talking to her like that, but I had to get her to open up while she was still unguarded.

The question hung in the air, then she said softly, "I don't know what I'm going to do. Just before he died, he told me he'd killed Dad for the jewelry shop. Ben, it's horrible. I can't tell anybody, I'm so ashamed."

"I can't imagine how you feel, but you've got to let Molly know what he said."

She whimpered softly, and I could barely make out her words. "I can't, not alone. It's too much."

"How about if I go with you?" I said. "I'll be there for you."

She nodded. "Thank you, Ben. I'm sorry for all of the mean things I said to you lately. I've just been under so much stress I can't stand it."

"Hey, you were just trying to protect your family. Let me call Molly and have her meet us at her office."

"Not the police station," Terri said, grabbing my arm tight enough to hurt. "I can't stand being around that many people right now."

"How about the garden at the soap shop? We'll have privacy there."

"That's fine," Terri agreed.

I dug out my cell phone and called Molly. Once she realized who it was, she was very curt with me. "Make it quick, I don't have time for you today."

Trying to keep my voice calm, I said, "I'm with Terri Joy. Her brother just died."

Molly hesitated, then said, "I'm sorry to hear that."

I continued, "Just before he passed away, he admitted to her that he killed their father. She'd like to talk to you, if you've got the time."

That got Molly's attention. "I'm in my office. Bring her straight here."

"She'd like to meet you at Where There's Soap. We're just about there. We'll be on the bench in the flower garden waiting for you."

"I'll be right there," she said, and hung up.

I pulled into the customer parking lot. It was closer to the garden, and it had the added benefit that Terri couldn't see the jewelry shop from there.

As we walked into the garden, she said, "Thanks, Ben, I can do this by myself now."

"I don't mind being there with you," I said.

"I need to tell this to Molly alone. Do you understand?"

"Absolutely. I'll wait right here for you, and when you're finished I'll take you home. We can get your car later."

"Thanks," she said as she put a hand on my arm. Terri started crying again, and I did the only thing I could think of. I put my arms around her and did my best to comfort her. I heard a car drive by the shop, and I looked up, fully expecting to see Molly.

Instead, Diana hesitated, saw me with my arms wrapped around another woman, then sped quickly away.

I was going to have some explaining to do, but it would have to wait.

Molly drove up a minute later. As she approached us, she asked, "Are you okay?"

"No, but I will be," Terri said.

The two of them walked toward the garden, and I could see Terri fighting another breakdown. Ten minutes later they approached me, and Terri said, "Molly's taking me home. Thanks, Ben, for everything."

I took her hands in mine. "If there's anything my family or I can do, don't hesitate to ask. You're not alone, do you understand me?"

She nodded, and Molly led her to her car.

After Terri was sitting inside, Molly turned to me and said, "Thanks for calling."

"Hey, it was my civic duty," I said.

She started to speak, then hesitated. "Listen, we need to talk. About a lot of things."

"I'm here whenever you need me," I said.

She smiled. "I'll take you up on that."

After they were gone, I stared at the garden, wondering what in the world I was going to say to Diana when she drove up and parked beside the shop.

"I was just getting ready to call you," I said.

She looked embarrassed as she said, "I acted like a schoolgirl running away like that. I don't know what got into me. We never claimed to have an exclusive relationship. Anyway, I just came by to apologize."

"Hang on a second," I said. "Don't I get a chance to explain?"

Her gaze stared downward. "I just told you, there's nothing we need to discuss. You're a free agent, Ben."

I gently touched her shoulder. "I want to tell you what happened. Terri Joy's brother just died, but before he did, he confessed to murdering their father. I was just trying to comfort her. There was nothing more to it than that."

Diana looked relieved by the admission. "Of course. I'm so sorry. I feel like such a nit," she said.

"I think it's sweet you care," I said. "Diana, there's something you should know about me. I don't date more than one woman at a time. It's just not in me. Right now, you're that woman, unless you're not happy with that arrangement."

She showed me how she felt by kissing me, long and hard. As we broke it off, I said, "I take it you approve."

Diana laughed as she got back into her car. "I've got to go open the bookstore."

"I'll call you later," I said.

When I walked back into Where There's Soap, my brothers and sisters were applauding, whistling, and stamping their feet. It appeared that Diana and I had had an audience without realizing it.

I took it for a few seconds, then said, "Okay, you've all had your fun. Now let's drop it."

To my amazement, they did just that. As the men drifted back to the production line, Kate and Louisa went back to their customers. At that moment, Cindy walked back in. "I heard you all from the parking lot. What did I miss?"

Before Kate or Louisa could say a word, I said, "Nothing much. Now that you're back, I've got some things I need to do."

"Where are you going?" Louisa asked me. "Andrew confessed to the murder. You're off the hook."

"There are still a few loose ends I want to tie up," I said. While I could believe that Andrew had killed his father, I was still puzzled by Ralph's behavior, especially with the coins I'd seen him intentionally tarnishing. Louisa was right. I probably should just leave it alone now that my name was cleared, but it wasn't in my nature. I wouldn't rest until I knew the answers to all of my questions, not just some of them. Andrew had told me he was going to Raleigh the night his father died. I'd assumed Molly had checked that alibi out, but it had to be faulty if Andrew found a way to get back and kill his father. Maybe he got to the hotel, checked in, and drove straight back. It was even possible he had someone else check him into his hotel. For whatever reason, he'd figured out a way to beat the system. That still left a lot of questions unanswered.

Where to go to get answers was another question entirely.

I thought I was driving randomly as I played with the possibilities racing through my mind, but I suddenly realized that my subconscious was working overtime when I found myself in front of the Joy household again. It was going to be a quiet place with Andrew and Earnest both gone. I got out and stared at the house, willing it to tell me its secrets.

Then I saw movement out of the corner of my eye. Ralph Haller, or whatever he wanted to be called, was coming out his own front door, a pair of suitcases clasped in his hands. As he threw them in the open trunk of his car, I approached on foot, but he didn't see me. I was almost to his front door when he charged back out, this time loaded down with boxes that had obviously been hastily packed.

"Going somewhere?" I asked him.

For a second I thought I'd given him a heart attack. His

face went ashen and the boxes slipped from his grip. "What are you doing here?"

"Did you hear about Andrew?" I asked, sidestepping his question.

"Yeah, I heard. It's a real shame."

I'd expected more of a reaction from him, especially given his previous devotion to Andrew Joy.

"That's all you've got to say about it?"

Ralph started retrieving objects from his fallen boxes. "What can I say? He's gone, but I'm still kicking."

"So where are you going?"

He said, "Out of town, out of Dodge, out of North Carolina, and if I don't do it soon, I'll go out of my mind. Does that satisfy you?"

There was definitely something amiss about his reaction. "Surely you're staying in town for the funeral."

"No way," Ralph said as he shoved a box into his backseat. "If I do, there might be two."

"What are you talking about?"

He shook his head. "You should have kept your big nose out of this. You're the reason he's dead."

"Andrew killed himself out of remorse," I protested.

"Yeah, right, that's exactly what happened." He hustled back into the house, and I thought about following him in when he came out, slammed the front door shut, and got into his car.

"You can't just run away," I said.

"Watch me."

He peeled rubber out of his driveway and raced down the road. Something had him spooked, and from the way he was acting, it was pretty bad.

I peeked inside his house, but there was nothing but

junk left behind. When I walked over to the Joy house, I thought about forcing my way in, but I knew all that would get me was a stay in jail. Molly was pretty serious about crimes committed in her jurisdiction and our history wouldn't save me from punishment if I blatantly broke the law. I went so far as to try the doorknobs, both front and back, but they were locked tight.

I couldn't do much if the answers were tucked away behind closed doors. I drove to the soap shop, then changed my mind at the last second and circled the block to the Joy jewelry store. No one was there, as I'd suspected, but there was a note on the front door. I got out and read it. CLOSED UNTIL FURTHER NOTICE was printed in bold letters. I wondered if the place would ever reopen. Terri was the only one left to run the jewelry shop, and she already had a job. She'd mentioned the possibility of running it herself, but I didn't see how she could do it now, given the circumstances. I peeked inside the window and looked at the display cases. Earnest really did have a fine touch converting old coins into jewelry. And then it hit me.

Old coins. Or were they? When I'd confronted Molly about Ralph Haller's counterfeiting conviction, she'd said it wasn't money, at least not any kind you could spend. I'd seen Ralph doctoring coins in his living room, and I naturally thought he'd been cleaning them until I'd talked to my brothers. Suddenly it all began to fit together. Ralph Haller had to be making counterfeit coins that Earnest was selling in his jewelry. If he wanted a bigger slice of the action, he could have killed Earnest himself. So why did Andrew's death send him scampering out of town like his tail was on fire? There could only be one reason I could think of. Someone else had killed Earnest, and Ralph must have suspected that they'd had something to do with Andrew's death as well. Who was left with motive, means, and opportunity? Then I realized how it all fit together. No one had heard Andrew's confession except Terri, the only other person in the world with motive enough to kill. By blaming her father's death on her brother, she'd made herself sole heir and put the blame on her brother. Then I realized that I'd given her the opening she'd needed at the hospital by asking her a leading question.

But how on earth was I going to prove any of it? I couldn't go to Molly. She'd laugh in my face. Kelly couldn't help me, either. I had to do something, but I couldn't imagine what.

Then I heard a car pull up behind the Miata, effectively blocking my escape route. It was Terri Joy, and she didn't look all that happy to see me.

"BEN, what are you doing here?"

I couldn't accuse her, but I had to get some evidence that I was right. "I was hoping someone would be here. I still need that present."

She raised an eyebrow. "Come on, that was a ruse, and we both know it. It's okay, I forgive you."

"You don't understand," I said. "Diana drove by when I was comforting you in front of the soap shop. I'm in hot water with her, and I'm hoping one of your pieces will help me fix it."

She looked sympathetic. "I suppose I should let you in, since I'm partially to blame. Come on."

I followed her into the store. I had a plan, but I wasn't sure it would work.

"So, have you come to any more conclusions about what she might like?" Terri asked as she dead-bolted the door behind us.

"I saw something the other day that would be perfect," I said.

"Pick out whatever you like, and I'll sell it to you at cost. I'm closing this place down, so it's time I got rid of our inventory."

"You're not going to run the store after all?" I asked.

"No, I never really liked retail anyway. I think I'll leave Harper's Landing altogether," she said. "There are too many memories here for me."

"I understand completely," I said as I moved to the case with the fake bar of gold in it. "I see just what I want."

I pointed to the display of ancient coins dangling from a necklace.

"I'm sorry," she said. "But I don't think so."

"I thought you said I could have anything I wanted?" I asked.

"Anything except items from that display." She reached into the case and pulled out the gilded lead brick with her left hand. "I'm sentimental, and these were the last pieces my father ever made."

I stared at her and realized I should have gotten Molly's help after all, even if it would have caused me some humiliation. "You're right. This isn't a good time after all. If you'll let me out, I'll go get her some flowers or something."

Terri nodded, and she followed me to the door. I had my hand on the dead bolt when I heard a click behind me. I didn't even have to turn around to know that she had a gun pointed at me.

"So, you know, don't you?"

"Know what?" I asked, refusing to turn around. Maybe I could bluff my way out of this after all.

"Give it up, Ben. It's no use. You always were too clever

for your own good. Now step away from the door and I may just let you live through this."

I pivoted, but realized the second I looked into her eyes that I wasn't going to get out of there alive.

"I give up. You're right, I know you did it. I just don't know why."

Terri laughed, but there was no joy in it. "And you think I'm going to tell you? Please, you're kidding, right?"

"Don't I deserve to at least know the truth?"

She shook her head. "Believe me, the truth is highly overrated."

"Humor me, Terri. After all, you won't be able to ever tell anybody else, and I've got a feeling I'm not going to live to see the sunset."

She appeared to think about it for a few seconds, then said, "Why not? It all started because of my moron of a brother. He never was very smart, but forcing Dad to commandeer your parking lot was a colossal blunder, and attention we didn't need."

"Why did he do it?" I asked, hoping against hope that someone would see our cars and wonder what we were doing in a closed shop.

"He found some of our coins in the backyard that Dad was trying to age naturally. It had been when he'd first gotten started, and he hadn't discovered that darkening agent yet. Dad forgot all about them, but Andrew uncovered them with his new metal detector, and he thought he'd struck it rich. If he'd just told Dad or me we could have set him straight, but he was too greedy. Andrew wasn't about to share."

"That's when he started gardening," I said.

"You've got it. He must have dug up a dozen old

spoons, buttons, and other worthless junk, but he was convinced there was more treasure out there. That's when he persuaded Dad to take over your parking lot. The fool even dug into it before I could stop him. I took Andrew aside and explained what we were doing, at least a part of it, and offered to cut him in. We'd been right to exclude him, though. When he found out, he threatened to go to Molly with the truth about our counterfeit coin scam. I decided he had to go, but then I saw a way to get it all for myself. If I killed Dad and pinned it on Andrew, I could inherit it all. But he left a clue before he died, and I didn't know about it until it was too late."

"Are you talking about the soap in his hand? I figure you planted that yourself to put the suspicion on my family."

She shook her head. "No, he did that himself. The clue wasn't the soap, though."

That's when it hit me. "It was in his left hand, and you were the only real suspect who was left-handed."

"Very good, Ben, but you're a little late." She laughed shortly, then added, "That's good. In a second, that's exactly what you're going to be; the late Ben Perkins."

I had to keep her talking. It was my only hope. "But what about Ralph?" I asked as I inched closer to the only weapon in sight, the gilded brick still on the counter.

"Who's going to believe an ex-con, especially when I had evidence to send him back to prison? He was leashed, good and tight. That's why he hated me so much. There wasn't a thing he could do to stop me."

"So you killed Andrew to cover up your father's murder," I said. I was almost there, and if she noticed me inching toward the brick, she didn't let on.

"I told him we'd claim his overdose was another murder attempt, and that would clear him forever with the police.

Andrew was almost grateful to swallow the pills and bourbon when I promised him I'd call an ambulance, so he'd be perfectly safe. At that point he was desperate to do anything to stay out of jail. I waited until he took the pills, and then slipped out the back. The fool came out of it long enough to call an ambulance, so I had to make sure he never woke up at the hospital."

"So you killed him again?" Okay, I knew it didn't make sense as I said it, but she understood.

"I would have if I'd had to, but he never woke up. No, Ben, I'm sorry, but the way I see it, you're my last loose end."

I saw her finger tighten on the trigger when I heard Molly pound on the front door.

"Drop it," she shouted.

Just as I grabbed the brick, Terri shot at me, and I thought I was going to die. The lead brick caught the bullet, though, and it was knocked out of my hand as it saved my life.

Molly put one shot into Terri's torso, and I knew that I wouldn't have to dodge any more bullets.

Terri Joy, like the rest of her family, was dead.

Thirteen

∘ ∘ ∘

"I've never been so happy to see you in my life," I said. "What made you come in?"

As she knelt down to search for a pulse I doubted she'd find, Molly said, "Some things didn't add up in Terri's story, so I wanted to ask her a few more questions. When I saw your car parked in the lot, I was ready to chew you out, but I guess you knew what you were doing after all."

I reached down and picked the brick up. "I got lucky, and I know it." I looked down at Terri. "She didn't want to go to prison, did she?"

"No, and it looks like she got her wish. Suicide by cop is the worst way to go. I didn't have any choice, Ben. I couldn't just let her kill you."

"Thank you, Molly. I thought I was going to die when I saw you through that door."

"I'd say you dodged a bullet here, but it's a little too close to the truth, isn't it?" She got on her radio and called in the death, and I stared into the display case. There were bodies everywhere, all because of one family's greed.

"Now tell me what you know," Molly said after she was through.

I brought her up to date, then said, "You've got to stop Ralph Haller. He was leaving town when I saw him half an hour ago, and if you can catch him, I'm willing to bet he's still got some of those coins on him."

She nodded. "I'll radio the state police. Why don't we wait outside?" Molly said as she looked down at the body.

I agreed, and we moved out to the parking lot. "Ben, are you going to be okay?"

"Once I catch my breath, I'll be fine," I said. "Molly, do you think I might be able to keep that lead brick?"

"That's a pretty gruesome souvenir, don't you think?"

"I don't think so at all. After all, it saved my life."

She nodded. "I'll see that you get it. Listen, there's no reason for you to hang around here. Why don't you go over to the soap shop, and when I'm ready for you, I'll come over there."

"Thanks," I said. "For everything."

"You're welcome," she said.

Since the Miata was blocked in, I decided to walk to Where There's Soap. I'd have to call Paulus and tell him it was safe to come home now, though I was tempted to leave him on Lois's couch for a while out of spite.

As I walked, I thought about how one family had been decimated by greed, a stain on the soul so deep that no cleaner on earth could wipe away its traces. My family had many flaws—no one knew that better than I did—but we loved each other, and in the end, that was really all that mattered.

Recipe for Basic Hand-Milled Oatmeal Soap

○ ○ ○

Oatmeal soap is a classic, known to soothe irritated skin.

INGREDIENTS:

- 10 ounces of grated soap or noodles
- 8 ounces of water
- ¾ cup oatmeal (long cooking or rolled oats only)
- chamomile, cary sage, or cinnamon (optional)

DIRECTIONS:

First, melt the grated soap with the water added in a saucepan.

Then grind the oatmeal in a blender or food processor until the flakes are about one-sixth of their original size.

Add the oatmeal and stir the mixture until it starts to thicken. The goal here is that you don't want all of the oatmeal to settle to the bottom.

After you've reached the desired consistency, it's time to add the optional fragrances if you'd like. Go with 8 drops of chamomile oil, 4 drops of sage oil, or a few drops of cinnamon.

Then pour your soap into molds. Wait until the soaps form a skim layer on top, then put them in the freezer. Check on them in an hour, then every half hour until they are solid. Freezing isn't absolutely necessary, but it usually makes the soaps easier to remove from their molds. After that, allow them to cure on an open-air rack for two to four weeks, turning them occasionally to allow for uniform drying.

Now it's time to put that new soap to use, so have fun with something you made yourself!

SOAPMAKING TIPS
FOR THE HOME HOBBYIST

○ ○ ○

HAND-MILLING soap is a great way to make a quality soap that can easily be tailored to your specific needs. Why go to the trouble of hand-milling? Many people find that hand-milled soaps have a more pleasing texture than soap that hasn't been ground. They last longer, and allow you to use fragrances and colors with a greater efficiency as well.

HAND-MILLING, also sometimes known as rebatching, simply means grinding or grating a basic bar of soap, then mixing it with water or milk, heating it, enhancing it, then pouring the finished mixture into molds. The tools needed are most likely ones you already own.

WHILE you can hand-mill your own soap if you'd like, soap noodles are readily available from most suppliers, and they make the process much easier. These noodles are made from soap that has already been grated, then extruded in a meat grinder and placed in plastic bags to retain moisture and workability.